# The Things We Did for Love

## Natasha Farrant

*faber and faber*

First published in 2012
by Faber and Faber Limited
Bloomsbury House, 74–77 Great Russell Street
London WC1B 3DA
This paperback edition first published in 2013

Typeset by Faber and Faber Ltd

Printed and bound by CPI Group (UK) Ltd, Croydon, CR0 4YY

A CIP record for this book
is available from the British Library

ISBN 978-0-571-27818-3

FSC
www.fsc.org
MIX
Paper from
responsible sources
FSC® C101712

2 4 6 8 10 9 7 5 3 1

For Justine and Lily, with love

# South-West France, 1944

France has been occupied by Germany since June 1940. For four years, she has had to pay for the cost of the Occupation, in money and in kind. A major proportion of her food and raw materials is taken by the occupiers while the French themselves go hungry. Young men and women are sent to work in German factories. A puppet government has been set up, French in name but taking orders from Nazi Germany. Its police, the Milice, work alongside the Gestapo to arrest any undesirables – Jews, Communists, Résistants – who are sent to concentration or death camps. As it becomes obvious Germany is going to lose the war, more and more people flock to join the Résistance and the Maquis, the underground army helping the Allies. The Nazi response to their activities grows more brutal: three men hanged for any German injured, ten for any killed. When the Allies land in Normandy on June 6th, the occupying forces, helped by the Milice, are quick to reassert their authority over the civilian population. Atrocities are committed in the name of maintaining the public order.

This book is based on one such event.

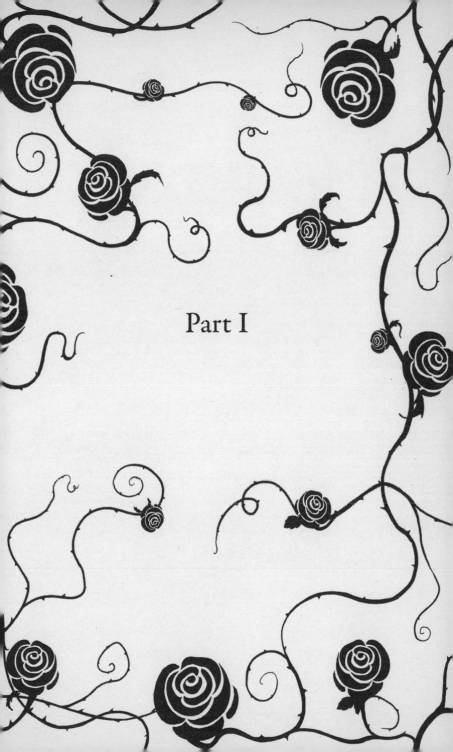

Part I

*I should leave. I want to – I think – but it's so difficult. I love it here. There's the lake, look, surrounded by trees. And there's the river going into it, where we used to swim because the lake is so muddy, and there's the road curving round the hill up towards the village. It's so peaceful. The countryside hasn't changed a bit. The river still gurgles, birds still sing. There's still wheat in the fields and deer in the forest, the hills still look blue where they meet the sky. Rain falls, sun shines. It looks so pretty, despite everything. Not exciting enough for a holiday, maybe, but you'd stop for a picnic in the woods.*

*Others stayed too, for a while. I've not been completely alone. Together, we pieced it all together. This is our story, but only I am left to tell it now.*

*So I'll get on with it, shall I? Then I can decide what to do.*

*Whether to go or stay.*

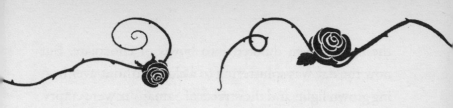

# February 1944

I

'Any minute now,' sighed Solange.

'I don't know why you're so excited,' said her cousin. 'I thought boys our age were all stupid.'

'This one's different.' Solange pulled a face, pretending to salivate. 'This one's new.'

'*Nearly* new,' corrected Arianne.

'Five years away makes him new,' said Solange. She rolled across the bed and pulled a nail file out of her bedside drawer. 'I wonder why they're coming back.'

'I'm sure we'll find out soon enough.'

'Mother heard there was a fight. She says they moved to his grandparents' at the beginning of the war because they were broke, but that his mother doesn't care how poor she is, she can't bear to live there any more. She says . . .'

'You shouldn't listen to gossip.' Arianne turned towards the window. 'People always exaggerate.'

It was still raining. Once, there had been fires and warm lights on winter afternoons, brioche straight from the baker's oven dunked into bowls of chocolate. But now the day was spluttering to a close without ever having grown light, and the streets of Samaroux were empty. The grates were cold to conserve fuel, the paraffin lamps used to supplement the electricity supplies were dim. As for brioche and chocolate . . . Arianne pressed her forehead to the glass and watched as a droplet detached itself from the top of the windowpane. She traced its course with her finger until it hit the water collected at the bottom of the glass. 'Imagine being that drop,' she said. 'To be all tiny and alone and suddenly to belong to a whole collective of drops.'

'You're so weird.' Solange had abandoned her nail file and was stuffing stockings down her bra, admiring her reflection in the mirror over her dressing table. 'You know what the problem is, don't you? Five years of war has made us dull. Nothing ever happens.'

'The Duponts came last year.' Arianne did not say what she wanted to say, that her father being taken prisoner had not been *nothing*. 'There are their piano recitals.'

'Piano recitals!' cried Solange.

'Paul says the oldest daughter can skin a rabbit almost as fast he can.'

'Your brother has the strangest reasons for liking people.'

'I've never known *you* turn your nose up at a rabbit stew.' Arianne turned to face the room. 'I don't think it is the war, you know. I think maybe Samaroux's too small for us. Maybe we should leave. Maybe . . .'

But Solange wasn't listening. She had joined Arianne by the window and was staring down at the street.

'Don't look now,' she murmured, 'but I think Samaroux just got bigger.'

And there below was Luc Belleville. Taller than when he went away, as skinny as they all were but broader than most boys his age, his jacket collar turned up against the rain. Five years . . . A group of women pressed around the cart which had brought him with his mother from the station to their old home across from Solange's house. Teresa Belleville embraced them each in turn. Luc ignored them, and began to unload cases from the back of the cart.

'Turn around,' urged Solange. 'Let us see you properly . . .'

'I wonder if they're back for good,' said Arianne.

'I do hope so,' drooled Solange.

Luc looked up. Arianne caught her breath. High cheekbones, full lips. Eyes which she knew from memory to be grey but which looked black in the half-shadows and which held hers for the space of a few seconds. She raised her hand in a half-wave. He scowled and turned away.

'Not fair,' cried Solange. 'Did you see how he looked at you?'

'He hardly looked at all,' whispered Arianne.

'Oh, he looked.' Solange bounced up and down, trying to attract Luc's attention, but he did not turn back. 'Believe me, he looked.'

They watched as the light from oil lamps moved from room to room in the house opposite, until Luc's mother leaned out to close the shutters.

'He knew we were talking about him,' said Arianne.

'Price you pay for a mysterious reappearance,' said Solange. 'And for being gorgeous.'

'Price you pay for living in a tiny village,' grumbled Arianne.

Solange spent the rest of the evening trawling through her wardrobe, trying on and rejecting outfits she knew by heart because when had she last had any new clothes? Arianne wrote in her diary, as she did every night, pages and pages, recording the minutiae of the day. *He looks just the same,* she wrote about Luc. *The same, but bigger. And FURIOUS. I know that look. He's spoiling for a fight.*

## II

Arianne had known Luc all her life, but the first time they met properly was on July 14th, 1939, Bastille Day, when he was eleven and she was ten.

The village picnic, as far as Arianne was concerned,

had been a disaster. She had looked forward to it since Easter and she had planned *everything*, from what she would wear to the games she would play with her friends when lunch was over. They were going to paddle in the river after lunch, then steal raspberries from Madame Lamotte's garden and eat them before tea. It was going to be *heaven*. Instead, when the time came, her mother was sick, her father would not leave her side, and she was saddled with looking after her brother.

'It's *so* unfair!' she complained to Solange. Paul, five years old and already a handful, was dissecting a cowpat with a stolen parasol. 'I still don't understand why Mother can't look after him. Or Papa. They might have kept him at home instead of inflicting him on me.'

Solange was silent, a reaction Arianne was growing used to whenever she complained about her mother. 'I suppose you think I'm being horrible,' she muttered. 'But it *is* unfair.'

'They'll bring pudding soon,' said Solange.

'I *always* have to look after him!'

'Chocolate éclairs,' murmured Solange. 'And meringues.'

'Yes, well. Meringues would be good.'

The afternoon was lifted by the promise of cakes. Games were organised, but when Solange rushed to join in, Arianne shook her head.

'I can't,' she grumbled. 'Because of Junior over there.

You go, though,' she added, with a generosity she did not feel. 'I know you want to.'

As Solange ran off, Romy Dulac detached himself from the crowd and began to limp towards Arianne. She groaned. Poor Romy, crippled by polio, with his three strapping brothers and his father so disappointed in him.

'He's like a dog,' she told her mother once. 'You know the way they sit and watch you when you eat?'

There wasn't a dog in all of Samaroux who couldn't melt Arianne's heart, but the thought of Romy's adulation today was too much. Paul was wandering towards the far end of the meadow. She jumped to her feet to run after him.

'Ari, wait!'

She hesitated, just too long, so that he knew she had heard him. Up ahead, Paul cackled and vanished into the long grass. She heard a splash, followed by a scream, and ran faster. Romy, helpless, watched her go.

She stopped short at the sound of laughter, her *brother's* laughter, an unmistakable sequence of gasps and chortles. The river bank was steep here. She walked to its edge and looked down and there was Luc, up to his waist in the river, messy blond hair pushed back from his face, spinning on the spot as he hit the surface with his palm. Drops caught the gold of the afternoon sun, and he gleamed in their reflected light. She wondered how she had never noticed him before. Luc, still spinning, sent a sheet of water over Paul paddling in the shallows. Paul squealed, looked up and saw his sister.

'Ari!' he bellowed.

Luc stopped turning.

'It was you,' she stammered, which in itself was strange. Arianne never stammered. 'The splash. I thought it was Paul falling into the river.'

'He wouldn't do anything so stupid, would you, Paul?'

Paul rolled on to his front, kicked his legs a few times and struggled to his feet. Arianne stared at him in awe.

'You're *filthy*!' she said.

'Cold,' remarked Paul.

'Out,' ordered Arianne.

'I've got a towel,' offered Luc. 'We can dry him on the grass.'

It was warm up on the riverbank. She fussed over Paul and tried not to look as Luc dried off in the sun. He was skinny but strong, his limbs tanned dark brown. He pulled his shirt back on but did not button it up, and the back grew damp where it touched his sodden shorts.

'*So* dirty,' she scolded Paul. She stripped him down to his underpants. He stood with his head down and his bottom in the air, preparing himself for a forward roll.

'He'll do that for hours,' she sighed to hide her blush.

'He's funny.' Luc held out a slab of chocolate. She

broke off a square and he took the rest of the row. 'I can watch him if you want to play.'

'You go. They were just starting a game of football.'

'Not today.' He had wolfed down his chocolate and now sat cross-legged on the grass, fiddling with a homemade catapult. 'Papa,' he explained. 'He used to say this picnic was the only reason he still lived here. I don't know why. All he did was drink too much then fall asleep by the river. But it still makes me think of him.'

He fitted a pebble to the catapult from a pile in his satchel and released it. The pebble smashed into a tree on the opposite bank.

'He made it for me,' he said. 'On this holiday, the year before he died.'

'Can I try?'

She fumbled her first attempts, but her fourth pebble flew straight. She had not anticipated the fun of it – the vibration of the catapult, the whistle of air, the sense of triumph when her missile slammed into its target.

'It's brilliant.'

'I'll make you one if you like.'

They played for a while longer, taking turns, until only one pebble was left. He nodded that it was hers and she took her time over choosing a target, enjoying the moment, the smoothness of the pebble, the unexpected companionship.

'Your mother's ill, right?'

She lowered the catapult.

'Sorry,' he said. 'Just I heard . . .'

'She's a *bit* ill.' Arianne raised the catapult again and squinted down her line of vision, aiming for a low stump with a bright patch of yellow fungus. 'But she's getting better.'

Luc said nothing. The fungus exploded.

'I have to go,' said Arianne.

'Ari.'

Strange, she thought, how her nickname on his lips sounded like a real name.

'If anything happens . . . I mean you know, if . . . Just remember I know what it's like?'

She nodded, not meeting his eyes. Paul had grown bored of his solitary games and they each took one of his hands, swinging him clear of the ground. As they walked back towards the picnic tent, neither of them noticed Romy watching from the trees.

∽

Arianne lay on her mother's bed that evening and told her about the picnic.

'I met this boy. Well, Luc Belleville. He was nice.'

'Surely you knew him before!'

'I knew who he *was*. I just didn't know *him*.'

'I taught him.' It was hard to believe Marielle Lafayette had once been a teacher, with her voice now little more than a whisper. She attempted a smile. Arianne looked away. 'Hopeless daydreamer. His father was a wonderful painter.'

'What did he paint?' Arianne turned on to her back and held her hands out above her face, gazing at the ceiling through her splayed fingers. She could imagine the paintings Luc might make. Green and gold, with bright splashes of colour.

'Landscapes, mostly. But always different. Like he didn't see them the way we did. Dancing. He made the countryside in his pictures dance. They were wild, but they had so much heart.'

'Dancing pictures!' Arianne snorted and flipped on to her side. 'Luc said he was going to make me a catapult.'

'That's nice too.' They lay in silence for a while. Marielle closed her eyes. Arianne stroked a strand of her mother's copper hair, the hair Paul had inherited, and noticed that it was streaked with grey. Elodie called her down for supper.

'I wish you could still cook,' she told her mother. 'Auntie Elodie's food is disgusting.'

Marielle's mouth twitched. 'It can't be that bad.'

'It is,' Arianne assured her. She leaned over to kiss her mother's cheek. 'I'll come back up after I've eaten.'

'And you'll tell me more about this boy.' Marielle squeezed her daughter's hand. 'This Luc.'

When she went up to see her again after supper, Marielle had pulled her blankets around her shoulders and lay as she always slept, curled on her side with her face resting on her hands, but Arianne could not wake her.

She didn't cry though. Not when her father broke down over Marielle's body, or when Paul crawled into her bed in the early hours of the morning, or even on the day of the funeral. They buried her late in the morning, with the sun already high in the sky and not a breath to ruffle the air. *He used to make the countryside dance*. It struck her that this was all wrong, that they should not be burying Marielle on a day such as this. They should have waited for a storm to play havoc with the trees and all this neatly combed hair, but they wouldn't. She had begged to keep her a little longer, but the answer – from the priest, from the undertaker, from Elodie and her father – was always the same. They *couldn't* wait.

They were throwing earth on the coffin. She closed her eyes, hoping this would drown out the awful sound of clods on wood. When she opened them she saw Luc Belleville, standing apart from the crowd, watching her. A feeling she didn't recognise began to swell in her chest, growing from the sharp-edged stone where her heart had been. It rolled through her veins and made her fingers tingle, raised the hair on her scalp, pricked her eyes and pressed at her throat. She doubled over, gasping. Somebody took her home.

Later, she found Luc in his mother's garden, working on a piece of wood with a knife. He wore nothing but a pair of ragged shorts and the sun cast dappled shadows over him through the leaves of a peach tree. *Dancing* shadows. He stood up as Arianne marched over to him. She slapped him and her hand left a mark on his cheeks.

'Again,' he said.

She flew at him with her fists. He wrestled her to the ground as she struck him and let her claw at him, her tears running off his skin into the hard-packed earth beneath them. They stopped fighting when she could no longer cry.

That was the last time she had spoken to him.

## III

'What happened was,' whispered Estelle Lafayette, Solange's mother, 'the boy was expelled from school, and the grandfather wanted to send him to work in Germany.'

'Oh no, dear,' said Bérangère Lamotte, the schoolteacher. 'I heard a quite different story. *She* wanted to get married – to a policeman!'

It was a few days after the Bellevilles' return from

the south, and Solange's parents had invited a group of neighbours for drinks to welcome the Bellevilles home. The guests of honour were late, and speculation was rife.

'You are quite absurd,' cried Madame Jarvis, who was the mayor's wife, and not above using her status to win an argument. 'It was the grandfather, all right, but it had nothing to do with the boy. What I heard was . . .'

The room fell quiet as Luc and his mother appeared.

'The door was open.' Teresa Belleville looked nervous but held her head high. 'We came straight in.'

'Say something,' muttered Solange to Arianne where they stood at the back of the room. She put her hand in the small of her cousin's back. 'Go on!'

'Why me?'

'Because I can't think of anything.'

'But . . .'

'Never mind, you're too late.'

Father Julien, the village priest, had broken out of the crowd and was walking towards Teresa and Luc with outstretched hands.

'My dear friends!' he cried. 'Welcome!'

'What I want to know,' whispered Solange, 'is how that man is able to stay so *fat*.'

'Don't be mean,' snorted Arianne.

'Excuse *me,* your Holiness. Well, will you look at that!'

Father Julien – who *was* fat, and jolly with it – was holding both Luc's hands in his, talking with him in a low voice.

'God,' breathed Solange. 'Luc looks like he's going to cry.'

'Shut *up*, Sol,' hissed Arianne.

'What's your problem? Oh right, they're coming over . . .'

'Do you know this splendid fellow?' Father Julien beamed as he reached the girls.

'Hello, Luc!' trilled Solange.

Luc nodded an acknowledgement.

'How was Aix?'

'Hot.'

He wore canvas trousers and a tight navy jersey. In the days when Arianne had pummelled him with her fists, his chest had been wiry and thin, no different from hers really, whereas now . . . His eyes were bright, a blaze of grey and gold. He asked her a question which she didn't hear. She managed a gasped *excuse me* and blushed.

'I said, have you had any good fights lately? Only, the last time we met . . .'

'Oh, *that*!' Her laughter sounded shrill and false. 'That was so silly.'

He looked disappointed. 'Not *really* silly,' she started to explain, but he had already moved on to the alcove at the end of the room where Paul, bored with the grown-ups, had taken refuge with Marie Dupont and her little sister to practise newly learned knots.

It was raining again. Arianne's face was still flushed. She slipped into the garden and raised her face to the sky.

## IV

A long way east, on the edge of a forest in Belorussia, it had started to snow.

In a stable on the outskirts of an empty village a bay gelding, once handsome but now too thin, pulled what hay it could out of its net. In a corner of his box, a man cowered, a greatcoat pulled over his massive frame. Night had fallen and so had the air temperature. The man shivered, pulled a bottle from the folds of his coat and drank.

'Alois?' Another man entered the stable, his frame slight in a captain's uniform swamped by a heavy wool coat, wisps of fair hair straying from beneath a bearskin hat. 'Alois, what the hell are you doing?'

'I didn't think it would be like that today,' whispered Alois.

'Well, no. Nobody ever does.'

Five hundred men jammed into open trucks. An

abandoned quarry, a line of guns, a gramophone record. Snow, always snow.

'Why did you play the music?'

The Captain shrugged. 'It helps. And opera seems the most appropriate.'

'It was awful.'

A cameraman waiting. The tailgate lowered. The order to jump and line up on the edge of the pit. The order to shoot.

'Did you see the first one?' whispered Alois. 'Little fat fellow with glasses who might have been your dentist?'

'I never look at their faces.'

'Captain Drechsler . . .'

'I'll tell you what, Alois, if your dentist really looks like that, you need to get a new dentist.'

'Are you married, Captain, sir?'

'Never found the right girl, Alois. You?'

'Yes sir. Married, with a little boy.'

'What are their names?'

'Clara, sir, and Wolf. I don't think they'd have liked what we did today.'

'It wasn't really you out there today, Alois. That's what you have to remember. We are no longer ourselves.So best not tell them, eh?'

'Are your parents alive, sir?'

'Pass me the vodka, soldier.'

'Are they?'

The Captain drank, wiped his mouth and drank some more.

'Yes they are,' he said. 'But I'm not going to tell them either.'

# March 1944

I

'Do you think we should go and see him?'

'And say what?'

'No, but do you?'

'God, Ari, you're getting boring . . .'

Tuesday afternoon, three weeks after the drinks party at Solange's parents. A geometry test to prepare for the following day, textbooks spread over the kitchen table and no revision being done at all.

'He's been back *almost a month*,' said Arianne. 'And I don't think I've heard him say more than a few sentences to *anyone*.'

'So he broods,' said Solange. 'It's part of his charm.'

Paul crawled out from under the table, making them both jump. 'He just thinks you're all stupid.'

Solange crowed with laughter.

'*That* was rude,' said Arianne.

'But it's true.' Paul rummaged through the bread bin, found an old crust and sank his teeth into it. 'He talks to *me*, but then I've got interesting things to talk about.'

'Like knots?' suggested Solange.

'He asked me about fighting,' said Arianne.

'Girls fighting!' scoffed Paul, and wandered from the room.

'That child is getting above himself,' said Solange.

'No, but do you think we should go?' asked Arianne.

Solange howled. Elodie, working in the vegetable garden, frowned. Paul, pulling on gumboots in the cloakroom, snorted. In the kitchen, Arianne cowered before her advancing cousin.

'You,' ordered Solange. 'Luc's house. Now.'

'But . . .'

'No buts. You're driving me crazy.'

'Come with me!'

'No way. I don't do mercy missions.'

'But I look . . .'

'Mad,' said Solange. 'Wild. You need a haircut and a whole new wardrobe, but I guess that's all to my advantage in the long run.'

'*Please* . . .'

'You're on your own, kid.'

Arianne's hand shook as she knocked at Luc's front door. She fought the urge to run away and pushed it open, then froze as it closed behind her. Luc and his mother were shouting at each other in the kitchen.

'You can't stop me!' she heard him yell.

'I'm your mother!' Teresa Belleville began to cry.

Arianne turned to go, but the door handle was stiffer on the inside than out and the sound of her fumbling echoed in the empty hall. The voices in the kitchen stopped. The door at the end of the passage flew open and Luc stormed out.

'You!' He looked furious. 'What the hell are *you* doing here?'

≈

'I wasn't eavesdropping,' stammered Arianne.

'You could have fooled me.'

The parlour into which Luc had dragged her was cold and dark. Arianne stood with her back against the wall. Luc paced up and down.

'I came to see if you were all right,' mumbled Arianne.

'Why the hell wouldn't I be all right?'

'Just, since you've been back . . .'

'What? What are people saying about me?'

'*Nothing*! It's just, you were nice to me when Maman was . . . when Maman was ill.'

'Oh, so you've remembered that now? It doesn't seem *silly*?'

'Excuse me?'

'Forget it.'

Luc moved away from the door and threw himself into an armchair. 'This place is unbelievable. No one seems to understand what it's like out there. There's a bloody war still going on and nobody seems to *get* it. All that *gossip*!'

Arianne thought about Elodie's daily battle to get food on the table, about Mayor Jarvis's grandson who never came back from fighting, about the farmer from the next village who had been shot for helping his three boys escape to England. *We understand*, she wanted to say. We understand more than you think. She opened her mouth to speak and found that her throat was choked with tears.

'Papa,' she whispered.

'Oh, give me a break.'

'*What*?'

'I'd rather my dad was in a prison camp than have . . .'

'What?'

'Nothing. Get out. I don't want to talk about it.'

ॐ

'How did it go?' asked Solange when she came round later that evening.

'Awful.'

'Are you all right?'

'I hate him!' Arianne pounded the counterpane on her bed. 'I hate him, I hate him, I hate him!'

Solange took her in her arms. Arianne burst into tears and told her what had happened.

'He's an idiot,' said Solange when Arianne had finished.

'I thought you liked him.'

'Not if he hurts you.'

'I never want to see him again.'

'That'll be easy,' said Solange. 'In a place this size.'

Little by little, Arianne's sobs subsided. 'I'm fine,' she mumbled at last. 'Really, I'm fine.'

## II

*Fine.* A word Arianne learned to use early. After her mother's death, to stop her father falling apart. When the news came that he had been taken prisoner and would not be coming home. *Fine.* Once, when Solange's mother had tried to make her talk, she had conceded *sad*, though it had seemed a poor little word to describe what she felt. *Like screaming* would have been better. *Dead. Terrified. Desperate.* On balance, *sad* had felt safer. And over the years, as all the bigger emotions had fallen away, sad was all she had left. Until that afternoon at Solange's window. And at the party, standing in the gold and grey blaze of Luc Belleville's eyes.

It was a week after her fight with Luc, and spring was returning to the woods around Samaroux. A pair of red squirrels flung themselves from branch to branch above her. Somewhere, hidden from view, she heard the warble of a thrush. This had been her mother's favourite time of year. The uncurling of hazel leaves, the footprints of a newborn fawn, the tender yellow of primroses. It had been impossible to walk in the woods with Marielle in spring because she was forever stopping to point things out. What had she called Luc? *A hopeless daydreamer.* She shook her head to expel the memory.

Arianne had walked fast, with little thought of where she was going. It wasn't until she reached a fork in the path that she realised she was almost at the old Lascande place. Her heart leaped. She had not been here for years, but a faded signpost confirmed that she was right. *Le Bos de Lascande, 0.5 km.* She closed her eyes.

Pigeons calling. A light breeze rustling the trees, and the rich smell of woodland humus. It could have been any time, but it was now. Arianne opened her eyes. She knew that she and her mother had been here once together. Old Madame Lascande had been a rich and fearsome woman, but she had liked Marielle. She invited her to tea sometimes, with instructions to bring all the novels she had most recently read, and she kept her there for hours discussing literature and philosophy. Once, she had ordered her to bring Arianne.

'You wore a red dress,' she told Arianne at Marielle's funeral. 'Only it was torn, because you tripped and fell.

You were quite out of breath, and crying. I gave you English Earl Grey tea on my terrace in rose-patterned tea cups, and some delicious biscuits.'

'I don't remember.'

'Well you ought to, you ate enough of them.'

*Did* she remember? The path joined a small road which wound its way through the trees to green-painted gates of elaborately worked iron. She gasped when she saw them. Was this a tug of remembrance or just the effect of the gates themselves, floating in the gloom of the woods, at once a barrier and an invitation? She pushed them. To her surprise, they swung open and she stepped on to a stone drive.

Yes, she *had* been here before. This was not just imagination or storytelling. The house, simple and low, built of local stone and yet somehow possessed of more elegance than any of the constructions at Samaroux – no one had ever described it to her but she recognised it, she was sure she did. There were shutters of faded blue, flower beds choked with weeds, a sweep as the drive opened into a courtyard, French windows giving on to a terrace, a front door shaped in a Norman arch. What had once been a lawn but was now more of a meadow, overgrown roses coming into bud . . . She *knew* it. Didn't she? She *remembered* it.

Arianne began to run. Halfway across the lawn she stretched her arms out at her sides and swooped like an aeroplane before spinning in circles. She reached the terrace, out of breath but still laughing, and threw herself to the ground by a wooden gazebo overgrown with vines. This was where they had taken their tea, she was sure of it. Madame Lascande and Mother had sat on this bench while she, quite recovered, played on the lawn. Arianne threw her arms around one of the gazebo's supporting pillars and pressed her cheek against it. Then froze.

Less than twenty feet away, standing in the late afternoon shadows on the edge of the lawn, was Luc.

## III

'Hands up, I admit it,' he said, when he had finally crossed the terrace to join her. 'I followed you.'

'But why?'

'You looked so purposeful. I wondered where you were going.' He frowned. 'What on earth were you doing just now?'

'I just came for a walk.'

'You were dancing. And laughing. And you just kissed that post.'

'I did *not* kiss it!'

'It was a little crazy.' He grinned. 'But also sweet.'

'I'm not crazy.' *And I am* not *sweet,* she wanted to add,

except that the words wouldn't quite come out. 'I was just . . .'

'Dancing, and laughing, and kissing wooden posts?'

'Exactly! That is what I was doing, because . . . because that is just what I wanted to do.'

'I get the feeling you always do exactly what you want.'

'Me?'

He looked embarrassed and she thought, *well, good!*

'So.' He sat on the wall which bordered the terrace and stretched out his legs. 'Do you come here a lot?'

'What is this, an interrogation?'

'More of an apology,' he admitted. 'For my behaviour the other day. Would you believe me if I said you were the only person I was looking forward to seeing when we came back?'

'Not from the way you behaved,' said Arianne.

'Fair enough.'

They sat for a while in silence. A bird sang out from the laurel hedge which bordered the garden. For a fleeting moment Arianne fancied it was calling to her.

'I usually walk the other way,' she said at last. 'I don't know why I came here today.' What should she say next? And how did one go from not talking at all to discussing such things? 'I was thinking about my mother,' she said. 'I came here once before, with her. It was like I was looking for her, like she was calling me, you know? And I was trying to find her.'

'I think I do know, yes,' said Luc. 'I feel the same sometimes about my dad.'

The light was behind him and Arianne could just make out her own reflection in his eyes.

'I'm sorry about your father,' he said. 'We heard, in Aix. I wanted to write, but I didn't know what to say.'

'Yes, well,' she said. 'You weren't the only one.'

'I heard you didn't talk to anyone for a year after he was taken prisoner. Is that true?'

Arianne shrugged.

'*Literally* nobody?'

'Except Paul.'

'What about school?'

'I wrote notes. It worked for a while, until they got annoyed and threatened to throw me out. I still don't talk much. Sol's always trying to make me.'

'Do you want to talk about him now? Your dad, I mean.'

'Not really.'

'Ah, go on. It's good to talk.'

'Coming from the champion of chat . . .'

He laughed. She relented.

'He's in a POW camp in the Jura, by the German border. He was interned just after the Armistice. We get postcards sometimes, and I write every Sunday but I don't think he gets all my letters. It's harder for Paul, he doesn't remember him so well. He's not been well. Papa, I mean. He had typhus but he's better now.'

'I'm sorry.'

Her nose was tingling.

'He was meant to come home,' she said.

'I know.'

'And then he didn't.' She sniffed. He nudged her and she turned away.

'The stupid thing is that he didn't have to fight,' she said at last. 'He was too old, but then he volunteered. He said he had to. He said he couldn't live with himself if he didn't.'

'Sometimes you just have to do things,' said Luc. 'He'll come back.'

'You think?'

'Sure I do.'

'I'm all right,' she said. 'It's just because you asked. Really, most of the time, I'm fine.'

'Ah,' said Luc. 'Fine.'

She let out a sob of laughter and sniffed again before looking up. His mouth twisted into a half-smile.

'Do you want to hit me?' he asked.

'No!'

'Well,' he said. 'That's a marked improvement.'

They sat in silence for a while longer, watching the shadows lengthen across the meadow.

'I'm still cross with you,' said Arianne. 'Just so you know.'

'Be careful, or I'll retract my apology. You *were* eavesdropping, technically. Also, trespassing.'

'I only came to say hello. And *technically*, are we trespassing now?'

'Where's the owner?'

'She went to America at the beginning of the war.'

'*Madame Lascande*? In *America*?'

'I know, Sol's so jealous. So, are we trespassing?'

'If the old lady's swanned off to America, I think we've every right to claim her house as ours.'

'The last time I came, it was all manicured lawns and tea parties.'

Luc laughed and stretched out beside her.

'Tell me about it.'

'I was very small.' She told him about drinking English tea on the terrace, Madame Lascande, the run through the wood and the red dress.

'It sounds idyllic.'

'I suppose it must have been. What were you and your mother arguing over last week when I was eavesdropping?'

'She doesn't want me to be a hero.'

'Do *you* want to be a hero?'

'Doesn't every boy?'

'I don't know. What will you do?'

He smiled. 'Free the world?'

'You could start by freeing my dad.'

They walked home through the sharp shadows of early evening and did not speak again until they reached the edge of the woods.

'Here we are, then,' said Luc.

'Here we are,' said Arianne.

'I'll see you around, I suppose.'

'I suppose you will.'

❧

She had algebra homework to finish that evening but the figures swam before her on the page. 'I can't do this,' she said at last.

'Do not give up,' threatened Elodie. 'You will never get anywhere without mathematics.'

*Where is there to get?* Arianne's retort was cut short by a knock at the back door. Elodie looked at the kitchen clock and frowned.

'It's almost ten.'

Arianne peered through the kitchen window. 'It's Luc!'

He didn't respond to her greeting when she opened the door, but thrust a makeshift parcel into her hands.

'It's a catapult,' he said. 'I was making it, the last time, when we had the fight. It's taken a while to get it right.'

He didn't wait for her to thank him but turned on his heels and vanished into the night. Arianne was still grinning an hour later when she went up to bed.

## IV

Luc had little time for his peers but he had taken to playing cards in the evening with a group of lads who had fought in 1940 and liked to talk about it when they drank.

'You should spend more time with your own crowd,' his mother complained. It was a fortnight after his meeting with Arianne in Lascande. They had just finished dinner and he was preparing to go out.

'I don't have a crowd.'

'You know what I mean. Boys your own age, boys in your class at school.'

She meant boys who wouldn't take him away from her at night, boys who didn't drink or sleep with their girl-friends, boys who were just that, boys, not young men itching for revenge.

'They don't get me.' He drained his water glass and carried his plate to the sink. 'Don't wait up, Maman.'

'Just . . .'

He rolled his eyes, but his face softened when hers contracted with misery. 'I promise I won't miss curfew.'

The Café de la Paix was crowded, as always. This was

where most of the villagers drank. The Bar des Sports, down the road, had been more popular before the war but since the Occupation there had been a clear split in the clientele: patriots on the one hand, profiteers on the other, if you believed the rumours. Walking in through a haze of cigarette smoke Luc clocked Father Julien playing dominoes with Mayor Jarvis and a couple of other old fogeys who had lived in the village since the beginning of Time – Gaspard Félix, the butcher, and Plonquet, the mechanic. A man Luc did not know sat at the table behind them, absorbed in a newspaper until Father Julien, spotting Luc, plucked it from his hands.

'Joseph!' cried Father Julien. 'Suppose I said I had found your baritone?'

The man called Joseph retrieved his newspaper with a tranquil smile.

'I should be delighted.' His voice was rich and deep, a curious mismatch for his small thin frame.

'Me?' said Luc.

'My boy, this is Joseph Dupont, a welcome addition to our little community since you went away. Joseph is thinking of starting a choral society.'

'Oh, no!' Luc backed away, laughing. 'I haven't sung for ages.'

'You always used to. I remember! In the church choir!'

'*Used to* being the operative words.'

'The ravages of puberty,' murmured Joseph Dupont. His lips twitched as he tried to suppress a smile.

'Sorry.' Luc grinned.

'I quite understand,' said Dupont.

'And that's it?' cried Father Julien. 'You're not going to press him? For all you know, the boy sings like an angel!'

'Have another drink, Julien,' said Jarvis, 'and shut up.'

'Man hath no greater achievement than that of making music,' grumbled the old priest.

'Which I wouldn't,' Luc assured him. 'Since my voice broke, I sound like a castrated cat.'

He smiled to himself as he walked through the low-lit bar towards the back, where the younger men sat. He liked Father Julien and the older crowd. His father had played dominoes with them too, sometimes, and taken him along for the ride.

'Watch it!' A tall, heavyset man cannoned into him on his way out and shoved him roughly aside. 'Don't you youngsters ever watch where you're going?'

'Speak for yourself,' muttered Luc.

'What was that?' The man curled his lip. His nostrils flared. His nose looked like it had been broken several times. Luc stepped back and held up his hands.

'I'm sorry I bumped into you,' he murmured.

'Like hell you are,' said the man.

'Who was *that*?' asked Luc when he joined the others.

'No one you want to know.' Thierry Legros, a farmer's son who had fought in North Africa, poured out a glass of beer from a jug.

'Jo Dulac.' Thierry's friend Marc was a mechanic and had served in the Air Force. 'Nasty piece of work. He's got a son your age. Rémy. Cripple.'

'Romy,' corrected Luc. 'And he's a year younger than me.'

'Ooooh,' said Marc's brother Jérôme. 'A whole year younger! That must make him, what – twelve?'

'Don't tease the kid.' Thierry picked up the deck of cards and began to shuffle. 'We're only just starting the game, thanks to our visit from the king of thugs there. What kept you?'

'Father Julien is looking for a baritone.'

'And he asked you? He must be desperate.' Thierry laughed and began to deal.

'What is it with those people and music?' mused Marc.

'What people?'

'People like Joseph Dupont.'

'I don't know what you mean.'

Marc rolled his eyes and whispered in his ear.

'Oh,' mumbled Luc. 'I didn't think.'

'That's the problem with kids,' sighed Marc. 'They never do.'

*They don't get me.* The phrase Luc had used to his

mother about his peers earlier in the evening came back to him as the game started. He looked round the table at these men he admired so much, and told himself that they viewed him as little more than a child, a sort of worshipping pet who kept them amused.

*She would understand me.* He knew it was true the moment the thought entered his head. He smiled, surprised at the relief of it.

'Penny for them.' Luc jumped as Thierry nudged him in the ribs.

'I'd put money on a woman,' said Marc.

'Either that or his Latin homework,' sniggered Jérôme. Marc roared with laughter.

'It's not like that!' said Luc.

'Then what's with the blushing?' Jérôme smirked as he picked up his cards. 'We won't tell her it's your first time . . .'

Luc blushed harder. 'It's not . . . I mean I don't . . . I just . . .'

'Come to the bar with me, kid.' Thierry was the kindest of the group, the only one Luc dared think of as a friend. 'Don't mind them,' Thierry said as they waited to be served. 'They're bored and frustrated.'

'Frustrated?'

'Sitting around on their arses, waiting for the Americans.'

'They could always join the Maquis.'

'You're right.' Thierry smiled. 'They could.'

'I wish *I* could do something,' sulked Luc. 'That would show them all I'm not a child.'

Thierry's smile grew wider. 'Tell me about the girl.'

'There is no girl.'

'My friend, there's *always* a girl. Who is she?'

'Arianne Lafayette,' muttered Luc.

'Nice!' whistled Thierry. 'But not easy.'

'I'm not interested in easy!' protested Luc. 'Look, she's not . . . I mean, in the south . . . I mean there *were* girls, right? Not lots, but more than one . . . This is different. She's had a hard time. I mean, with her parents and everything.'

'We've all had a hard time, my friend. One way or another.'

'I want to make things better for her.' Suddenly Luc knew exactly what to do. He grabbed Thierry by the sleeve. 'I need to get hold of some stuff. Can you help?'

'What stuff?' Thierry frowned as he listened, then started to chuckle.

'I know exactly who you need to talk to,' he said. 'Though she probably won't thank you if she ever finds out.'

'I don't do fancy goods anymore,' said Paul. 'Not since the last time.'

'Come on, mate. It's for your own sister.'

The boy seemed to have grown in the few minutes since Luc asked him for help. He had found him oiling rabbit traps at the bottom of his garden with Marie Dupont, and though Paul still sat cross-legged on the ground his back was straighter than it had been before, the tilt of his chin more pronounced.

'But what's the point?' he asked.

'I know what I'm doing.'

Paul sniffed and picked up another trap, then put it down again to unbutton his shirt.

'Look.' He pushed the fabric away from his shoulder. His right upper arm was vivid with red and purple fingermarks.

'Jesus, Paul! What happened?'

'He got caught,' murmured Marie. 'A chocolate delivery to a big house in town. Paul, I don't think you should do this.'

Paul shrugged back into his shirt and grinned at Luc. 'What a waste of time *that* was. Posh cow I was delivering to never even paid my train fare. Not that I ever *buy* a ticket.'

'I'd have paid your train fare.'

'Sure you would.'

'I've got cash.'

Paul's eyes gleamed. 'How much?'

'Enough to make it worth your while.'

'You promised your sister you would stop,' said Marie. 'Actually, you also promised *me*.'

'It'll cost you,' said Paul.

'That's fine.'

'If Ari finds out you used me, she'll never talk to either of us again.'

'I promise she won't find out.'

'Give me a week.' Paul had finished polishing his traps, and jumped to his feet. Standing, he looked small again. Luc had a moment of misgiving. 'If you do anything to upset her,' said Paul, 'I will kill you.'

And so now here he was. Back at Lascande, hiding under the gazebo on the little terrace, trying to calm his unfamiliar nerves as he waited for her.

There had been two girls in Aix. The first, Marine, was the older sister of a schoolfriend, not long widowed, who took him to bed one afternoon then burst into tears and never spoke to him again. He didn't remember the second one's name. He'd gone to her to get Marine out of his head, and left vowing he would never pay for it again. This was different. This was . . . he couldn't put his finger on it.

Here she was now, standing on the edge of the lawn.

A curtain of clematis fell from the wooden beams of the gazebo, hiding him from view. He parted it, just enough to take aim with the catapult he pulled from his pocket. A pebble flew across the grass and landed a couple of metres away from her. He felt a pang of remorse at her scream, then chuckled when she crouched to examine his projectile. The next pebble landed at her feet and this time he heard her laugh.

'You can come out now!' she called. 'I've got your little game.'

He didn't show himself, but watched her pick her way across the overgrown grass towards him. She had changed out of her usual skirt and jersey into a light green dress cinched at the waist with a red belt, and she had pinned up her hair. She looked very confident as she made her way towards him but she hesitated when she reached the clematis. The feeling he couldn't identify earlier swept over him with renewed force.

Tenderness.

'I know you're in there,' she said, and pushed the curtain of flowers aside.

A wooden tray, painted white. Rose-patterned china – plates, tea cups and saucers. A matching bowl with cubes of sugar and tongs of filigree silver. Round thin biscuits yellow with butter, slices of lemon, a teapot with steam curling from its spout. He had set it all out on a low table spread with a linen cloth.

'Well?' he asked. 'What do you think?'

She dragged her eyes away from the table to look at him. 'It's perfect.'

'Just as you remembered it?'

She smiled, hesitantly. 'The company's different. No, it's all right!' She stretched out her hand. He noticed that it was small and white, and that she bit her nails. 'I was just saying.'

'In that case . . .' He jumped to his feet, picked up a plate and held it out with a flourish. 'Would Mademoiselle care for a biscuit?'

After tea, they lay on their backs on the lawn.

'I feel a bit sick,' she confided. 'I'm not used to sugar any more.'

'Nice, though.'

'Definitely nice. Wherever did you get it all?'

'Just people I know.'

She propped herself up on one elbow and raised an eyebrow.

'All right.' Luc grinned. 'People who know people I know . . .'

'I'm surrounded by bandits.'

'Is that a good thing?'

'As long as they don't get caught.'

She wouldn't meet his eyes, and her neck had gone pink. He jumped to his feet and held out his hand. After a moment's hesitation, she took it.

'Come,' he said. 'Let me show you the rest of the house.'

## VI

She tried not to stare too obviously as he knelt before her to pick the lock. The back of his neck was brown, softer than the rest of him, with short hair curling on the sides.

'Classic three-lever mortise,' he boasted. 'Last time it took me less than two minutes.'

'What is that thing you're using?'

'Curtain pick.'

'A *curtain* pick?'

'A bolt thrower, if you prefer.' He winked. 'Call it a tool of the trade.'

'I don't think I'm ready for a life of crime.'

'Sshh . . .' The ring handle clunked. 'We're in!'

The scullery smelled of mildew. Arianne shivered on the threshold.

'Breaking in so easily,' she said. 'It could make a girl think.'

'Think what?'

'Think twice.' She pushed past him into the house.

She remembered nothing of the scullery or its attendant passageways, which were stone-floored and white-washed, with doors into larders and pantries, washrooms and store cupboards. 'It's not so surprising, though,' she said. 'I was very small, and I suppose this *is* the servants' part of the house . . .'

'This is where I found the tea things.' He held open a door into a pantry stacked from floor to ceiling with chinaware.

'Clever of you to pick the right set,' said Arianne.

'There's only one with roses.'

'Even so.'

She picked up a bowl and shook out a handful of mouse droppings.

'Nice,' said Luc.

They left the china pantry and pushed through swing doors into the kitchen. The air here smelt sweet. A bunch of herbs had been hung to dry from the massive crossbeam which supported the chimney breast: sage, rosemary, thyme and bay. Arianne buried her nose in it and memories of other meals came back to her, eaten in other houses, before rationing took all the pleasure out of food.

'I'm hungry again,' she sighed.

An oak table, scrubbed of colour, occupied the centre of the room. She spotted a dog basket in the far corner with a rug folded over it, and an overstuffed armchair with broken springs. Cooking pans hung from hooks over the range, and a pile of dishcloths sat on the draining board, as if waiting to be put away.

'Are you sure no one lives here?'

'There's no sign of them if they do.'

She followed him out of the kitchen. The living room smelt of woodsmoke and beeswax. She flung herself into a dust-sheeted armchair.

'You could make me more tea.' She grinned. 'And bring me biscuits.'

'Who are you, the Queen of England?'

They took the stairs at a run, their wooden soles clattering on the stone steps. Upstairs, an empty corridor ran the length of the house. Its floor, made of the same light stone as the stairs, gleamed in the half-light which streamed through the louvred shutters of the casement windows.

'I'm going to open them,' announced Luc.

She left him to it and began to open doors on to a series of rooms, all different and yet, with their stripped and covered furniture, all very similar. She turned back to Luc. The forest through the open windows looked close enough to touch.

'It's like Hansel and Gretel,' she said. 'The house in the woods.'

'It's hardly gingerbread. And there's a distinct lack of witch, unless there's something you haven't told me?'

'You know what I mean.'

She opened another door. 'I just found the giant's bathtub.'

'Here's another bedroom.'

'Another one!'

'This one's amazing.'

The room at the end of the landing was painted an old rose pink, with views over both sides of the house. The furniture here had not been covered. Four gilt-framed armchairs stood around an inlaid table before one of the windows. The bed, a four-poster, was hung with green velvet, the mattress covered with a matching counterpane trimmed with gold brocade.

'I can't work out if it's spectacularly vulgar or actually quite enchanting,' said Luc.

'A bit of both, I think,' said Arianne.

She sat on the edge of the bed and felt the velvet slide beneath her fingers. Luc stood with his back to her, silhouetted against the light, but in her mind's eye she saw a different figure bending over her, recalled the smell of antiseptic, pressure as a plaster was applied to her knee. Someone else hovered in the background, a white dress, a blaze of copper hair. She closed her eyes again, willing her mother's shadow to come forward but it was no good and she fell back against the cushions.

The bed's canopy was panelled and each panel bore a different carving – grapes, a flower, a sleeping cat.

'Still thinking you're the Queen of England?' Luc had turned and was looking at her.

'I was wondering who would make a bed like this. Also what it would feel like to sleep in it.'

'You could always stay and find out.'

'It wouldn't feel right.' She left the bed and began to walk round the room, trailing her fingers over the dust-coated furniture. 'They brought me up here when I hurt my knee. Madame Lascande gave me a sticking plaster.'

'I'm not sure I can recreate that for you.' He smiled as she came to stand before him in the half darkness.

'The tea party was quite enough.'

'Did you like it?'

'I loved it.'

'I'm glad.'

Everything in that room was filtered. Light, sound, even space seemed to contract so that Luc felt much closer to her than he was. Her breathing became difficult again.

'We should go,' said Luc.

❧

Her face, the way it glowed in the half-light! He had to tell her. If she was to understand him, she had to know the truth.

She waited outside while he shut up the house.

'Hold out your hand,' he said when he joined her. 'And close your eyes.'

49

Her eyelids were so smooth they didn't look real. Her lashes swept the top of her cheekbones. She opened her eyes as soon as he dropped the key into her outstretched hand.

'I found it hanging in the kitchen.'

'I shouldn't take it.'

'You have to, it's a present.'

They set off together towards the drive.

'Why did you do it?' she asked. 'The tea party, I mean.'

'To make you happy, of course.'

She looked pleased but puzzled.

'I just wanted to,' he said.

The shadows were lengthening and the light in the woods was veering to blue. Birds sang all around them, trying to hold on to the dying day. He cleared his throat. He had to tell her, *now*.

Arianne walked beside him, lost in thought but looking happy.

'I suppose you have heard all sorts of stories about why we came back,' he said.

'Excuse me?'

'You have to promise you won't repeat this.'

They had reached the old signpost to Lascande.

'Let's stop here.'

For a moment he feared she would not stop. He was struck by the irrational fear that if he let her go now he would never see her again. She would walk out of his life down the green twilit path, away from him and his untold story, and the last good thing in his life would be lost.

Arianne placed a hand on top of the signpost, walked around it slowly, came to a halt just before him and smiled.

'I promise,' she said.

He swallowed. 'On second thoughts, let's walk.'

*Courage*! he told himself, and began.

'You know we went to stay with my grandfather when the war started?'

'Everyone knows that.'

'For the last two years, we had these German officers staying with us, pretty high-ranking ones. They kicked us out of all the good rooms so we had to move up to the attic. Maman and I tried to ignore them but Grandfather was so desperate to do the right thing, I mean for them to *see* he was doing the right thing. He even locked me out at night if I was late. He told them there was a curfew and I had to learn. That's when I learned to pick locks.'

'How awful,' she said, but he could hear her thinking *is that all?* He pressed on.

'They brought him presents. Coffee, sugar, cigarettes – you know the sort of thing. One of them spoke pretty good French. He was really into Napoleonic history, just like Grandfather, which got him all into thinking you know, they're not so bad, we're lucky, look at Poland. I think – well, Maman thinks – it made him feel better about what happened afterwards. After a while they started to ask him for information. There was this family living in our street, they'd been there since the beginning of the Occupation. Two parents and a little girl, Jewish. False names and everything, we found out afterwards. Anyway one morning we woke up and they were gone.'

'Oh,' said Arianne quietly.

'Yes,' said Luc. 'Oh.'

'Where did they go?'

'Where do people ever go when they disappear, Ari? He couldn't see that he'd done anything wrong, denouncing them. Said that this was France, nothing bad would happen and that anyway it was because of people like them there was a war in the first place. He got a whole carton of cigarettes for them. He tried to give some to Mother, but she threw them back in his face.'

'How did that go down?'

'He said she was obviously a communist and he never wanted to see her again.'

'Your poor mother.'

'She was shaking afterwards. It was so unlike her to answer him back. Afterwards she wouldn't stop crying but we left within twenty-four hours. She still cries all the time. It drives me nuts.' He stole a sidelong glance at her. 'I know that sounds harsh. I just don't know what I can do. She's started going to church again, which is good except she's planning this weird memorial mass for my father. I mean, he died over seven years ago, and he *never* went to church. I think it's all part of her rebelling against Grandfather – he hated Papa. Honestly, life at home . . .'

'What?'

'Oh, nothing. It's just heavy. And I can't stop thinking about the little girl they took away. I can't get her out of my head.'

They had stopped where their paths parted by the edge of the wood. Luc scuffed the ground with his foot.

'You did say, if I wanted to talk.'

'I'm glad you told me.'

'Remember when we fought? It started something, didn't it?'

'Yes,' she said. 'It did.'

'Are you shocked?'

'Those poor people.'

'You promise not to tell.'

'Of course!'

'Right then.' He hesitated. 'I'll see you in school.'

'Luc?'

He turned back. He could hardly see her in the shade of the wood.

'That last room. Why do you suppose they left it uncovered?'

His answer slipped out before he even had time to consider it.

'For us,' he said.

# April 1944

I

Alois Grand had taken to writing letters and burning them. The Captain was right, he didn't want Clara to know, but it helped to feel he was talking to her.

'*Today was difficult*,' he wrote. '*Today there was no time to sort them, the ones who should die from the ones who should have lived.* God will know his own, *the Captain said, which is something a French bishop said, apparently, when he had the same problem. We don't line them up any more, the Captain doesn't like it. He says there's no sport in it and we have to give them a chance*.'

There wasn't much sport Alois could see in shooting unarmed civilians as they ran to escape an enclosed space in the dead of winter, but the Captain insisted. 'There's always a way out. If they make it, we let them go.'

'If you let them go, they'll freeze.'

'*We have a job to do*,' Alois wrote. '*To rid the Eastern territories of Jews. Jews and Communists. Jews, Communists and anyone else who disagrees with us. The Captain goes on about the survival of the fittest. The local militia did it for us at first but he doesn't trust them any more.'*

It was one way of coping, Alois supposed, turning the whole campaign into a game. They all had their ways of dealing with it. Transfers, suicides. Just getting on with the job.

'You might as well,' reasoned the Captain. 'Someone else will only take your place if you don't. If you refuse, I might even have to shoot you.'

'Would he do that?' asked one of the newer recruits.

'Oh yes,' said Alois.

Given the choice – which he wasn't – he preferred the pits. March them out, shoot them in. Don't look, don't listen, shovel over earth or lime and leave. At least it was efficient. Letting them make a run for it was messy. Men, women, old people, kids – none of them stood a chance but it didn't stop them trying. He sometimes wished one of them would stand still but they always ran, and the gathering of their bodies afterwards was gruesome.

*'Today a child did get away. We were in a clearing in the forest. Two machine guns, ten rifles, two dozen villagers at a time. More of a battery farm than a hunt. He was a skinny child, about Wolf's age. He made straight for the trees. We all saw him, but he was so damn quick. We didn't talk about it, but I think we were all glad.'*

⁊⁊

The child did not make it far. The Captain returned from his morning hunt the next day to tell them he had found his frozen carcass curled like an animal beneath a shrub. One of their comrades, a former schoolteacher, went into the forest and shot himself. *Daft,* said the Captain, and *daft*, Alois agreed, because it didn't do to contradict the Captain. *I am only obeying orders,* he wrote to Clara. *But I'd like to come home now.* He burned that letter too.

## II

Paul had been trading in information ever since his sister returned from her tea party at Lascande, but he was growing weary of it.

'No, they haven't kissed,' he sighed.

Romy Dulac squirmed.

'How can you be so sure?'

'If they'd kissed, she would be unbearable. She's only just possible to live with as it is.'

'But they're so often together.'

'All moony and dreamy and locking herself in her room . . . Sol's with them a lot, you know. And when they're alone, like when they go for walks and things, they just talk. They don't even walk close together. Once I saw his arm brush hers, and she jumped like a scorched cat.'

'You're sure there's nothing else?'

'His mother's happy because he doesn't go out so much to play cards. Sometimes she goes to church with my Auntie Elodie, and *sometimes* he wears blue-striped underpants with purple spots. Look, I don't want to be rude, but can you pay me now?'

A flicker of panic crossed Romy's face, and he pulled a handful of coins from his pocket.

'I'll double your money for some proper dirt on Luc.'

'Triple it,' said Paul.

❧

Romy had been in love with Arianne for seven years and eight months. He would never forget it: eight years old, morning break. Two weeks into the first term of a new year and he was already hiding from bullies. No matter that he had grown over the summer, that an operation on his club foot had reduced his limp, that his mother had defied his father and bought him less hideous spectacles. Eric Lherbe and his gang of thugs still made his life a misery, until *she* caught them at it. Fierce and tiny, her curls sticking out like a dark halo around her head, she retrieved his exercise book from the toilet, kicked Eric in the balls, elbowed one of his henchmen in the ribs and, in a tone he later recognised as her great-aunt's, told them that they should be *ashamed of themselves*.

'You were incredible!' cried Romy as the bullies ran away. In the ardour of his admiration, he forgot to feel ashamed. An image came to him, recalled from a history book, of a girl in a suit of armour on a white horse. 'Like Joan of Arc!'

Arianne looked horrified.

'Without the burning, obviously,' he tried to explain, but as she swept away from him, her victory won, he was certain of two things: that he loved her; and that, to her, he was nothing.

Her indifference hadn't mattered until now. After the news came about her father, when she spoke to nobody but her brother, he waited for her every morning and walked her to the station in silence. When other friends turned away, defeated by her unhappiness, Romy remained faithful. He left flowers for her on her birthday and brought chocolate every Easter, he wrote poems he never showed her. Over time, he liked to think he had tamed her. She began to smile at him when she came out on school mornings, and shortened her stride to match his limp. Sometimes, when his father's temper made him late, she waited for him. Once, when it was obvious he had been crying, she had pressed his arm to show she understood.

It was not much, but it had been enough.

But now *he* was back and she never waited any more.

'She has a copy of his timetable,' said Paul. 'Sometimes she goes in early just so she's on the same train as him. Sort of accidentally on purpose. He does the same thing. I know,' he added, not without arrogance, 'because it was me who got them the timetables.'

'Well, get me one too.'

Monday morning, and he set his alarm clock early, bolted breakfast and set off down the footpath which led from his house to hers. He did not have to wait long. She flew out of the house as the church clock chimed the half-hour. She was wearing a pink dress which he was sure had once belonged to her cousin – Solange had caused a sensation almost falling out of it at a picnic last summer, but it looked different on Arianne's slight figure. Her hair was tied back again, a new style for her which showed off the heart shape of her face and made her eyes look bigger. It suited her, though he missed the old tangles.

She swung into the lane and he tried not to mind that she did not even look to see if he was waiting.

'Ari!'

'Romy! I didn't see you!'

'Class doesn't start till ten today. Didn't anyone tell you? Maths teacher's away again.'

'I know, I've . . . I'm working on a project. I need the library.'

'I'll walk with you.'

'Why are you going so early?'

60

'I, oh. You know. Things to do.'

He should tell her now, while they were alone, but he could not think how to do it. He could barely speak, anyway. She made no allowances today for his leg and he panted just to keep up with her.

'Why don't you slow down and get the next train?' she asked.

'It's not a problem.' He grimaced a smile. 'What's the project?'

'Excuse me?'

'You said you were working on a project.'

'Can you *really* not walk any faster?'

They turned the corner into the main street and there he was. Leaning against the station wall, dark blond hair pushed back from his face, schoolbag flung over his shoulder. Arianne's face lit up. Romy walked on, exaggerating his limp, forcing her to slow to his pace.

'I suppose you heard about his grandfather?'

The way she froze, the way she wouldn't look at him – she knew already! For the first time since Paul delivered his information, it occurred to Romy that in muddying Luc's name he wasn't doing himself any favours either.

Once his father had shot a doe out of season. The fawn standing over her mother's body looked just as Arianne did now.

'I don't know what you mean,' she stammered.

'It doesn't matter.'

'You wouldn't have said anything if it didn't matter.'

'Drop it, Ari, all right?'

'No.' Her shoulders were squared now, her chin raised. 'I want to know what you meant.'

'I think you know what I meant.'

'I don't know why it matters,' she said. 'I don't know why you even care.'

'It mattered if he hadn't told you,' he sighed.

They had almost reached the station. Arianne turned to look at him, and there was not a trace left of the stranded fawn. 'I don't know how you found out,' she hissed, 'but if you breathe a word of this to anyone, I'll make your life hell, do you hear?' Her eyes blazed at him. 'People in glass houses, Romy. People in glass houses.'

She hated him, and the worst of it was that he could see why. Luc was peeling himself away from the wall, glancing from Arianne to Romy. Romy could have cried.

'Better hurry,' said Luc. 'Train's due any minute.'

She walked between them, but her eyes kept sliding towards Luc. Romy thought he had never seen her like this, so coiled and tremulous, like a bird about to sing or a cat before it pounced. They paused to cross the road. Luc slipped a hand beneath her elbow – did it with such ease!

If he said anything, he would lose her. But he had lost her anyway.

'We were just talking,' he said, 'about your grandfather.'

## III

Solange joined them on the train. Luc didn't speak a word until they arrived at Limoges, where he gripped Arianne by the arm and pulled her roughly aside.

'How *could* you!' he exploded.

'It wasn't me!'

'I trusted you!'

'Romy . . .'

'Do you *know* what his father is?'

'I don't know how he found out, Luc, I swear!'

'They say he's turned more people over to the Gestapo than anyone in the area.'

'You're hurting my arm,' said Arianne.

'Draft dodgers, black marketers – people like Thierry, like your own *brother*, for God's sake. Imagine if Paul was older! Thierry's only around because he bribes that scum. And you go blabbing to his son!'

'I did not blab!'

'You were gossiping about me!'

'You're just as bad as everybody else,' she shouted as he walked off. 'You think you're better, but you're not.'

'*What?*'

'You're so afraid people will judge you because of your

grandfather, but you're very quick to tar Romy with the same brush as his dad.'

'It's not the same.'

'Isn't it?'

Luc looked furious. Arianne began to shake.

'Come on, Ari.' Solange had been waiting a small distance away and stepped forward now to take her cousin's hand. 'We'll be late.'

Arianne burst into tears. Luc's expression softened, then set again into a hard line beneath Solange's reproachful gaze.

'I don't want to talk to you any more,' he said.

'That's fine by me,' sobbed Arianne. 'I never want to see you again either.'

∾

She guessed what had happened that afternoon, as soon as she discovered that the pagemark in her diary was missing.

'You monster!' she yelled. Paul was sitting on the floor of his bedroom, counting cigarettes. She waved the diary in his face. 'You little toad!'

'I don't know what you're talking about.'

'I'm talking about the ribbon – mother's ribbon – that I always keep in my diary. I'm talking about the sordid little deals you've been cutting behind my back.'

He managed to hold her gaze. 'It's called the free market.'

'No it's not! It's called betraying and cheating and stabbing people in the back. It's called having no honour or scruples or integrity!'

'I don't even know what any of those words mean!' he said sulkily.

'Exactly! You're wild, and you're becoming horrible. You would never *dare* behave like this if Papa was here!'

'Well he's not, is he!' Paul shouted. For a moment, he looked like he was going to cry. 'He's not here, and neither is Mother!'

He threw his cigarettes to the floor and bolted from the room.

'I haven't finished with you yet!' she roared.

She caught up with him at the back door and grabbed his arm.

'Let me go!' he yelled.

'I'd like to whip you!'

'Well, you can't!' He wrenched himself free and ran out into the garden. 'I hate you! I hate all of you!'

೨⊙

Nobody ever went in to her father's study except for Elodie, and even then only to dust. Arianne entered it now as she would a shrine. Nothing had changed. There was still the same framed photograph of the four of them on the mantelpiece, her mother radiant and healthy, Paul no more than a toddler, she with braids hanging over her shoulders. The papers he had left on his desk lay under the stone paperweight she had once painted for him, the book he had been reading sat on the same table. *Ready for me to pick up again when I come back,* he had said. She threw herself into his favourite of the two armchairs before the fire. The leather smelt of his pipe.

She was still shaking from the argument with Paul.

'You have to come home now, Papa,' she sighed out loud. 'I don't think we can manage without you any more.'

She stayed until the light outside grew dim. She thought about lighting a fire and maybe sitting at the desk to write, but it would have meant disturbing the fragile balance of the room, and so she did nothing. In due course, she became aware of voices in the kitchen. Somebody was crying. She roused herself and tiptoed down the hall to listen.

Through the half-open door she saw Elodie, regal despite her bedroom slippers, hovering over a boiling kettle. Luc's mother sat at the table.

'I'm so sorry,' said Teresa. Her voice quivered, and her face was puffy from crying. 'I didn't know where else to turn.'

The kettle whistled. Arianne strained to hear, but caught only isolated words. *So ashamed . . . so angry . . . everybody knows . . .* Was she talking about Luc or about herself?

Elodie turned, holding a pot full of limeflower tea, saw her great-niece and frowned. Arianne raised her hands and backed away. She didn't go down to dinner that night but stayed in her room, pretending to be ill. Later, when the others had gone to bed, she stole back down to the study and took the family photograph. She put it on her bedside table and fell asleep still looking at it.

∞

'I don't actually care,' she told Solange over the days that followed, when Luc still wouldn't talk to her.

'Right,' said Solange. 'You don't care.'

'Just, we were friends. He was different.'

'He's different all right. Flying off the handle like that. I've gone right off him.'

'He's proud!'

'Oh, proud,' mocked Solange. 'I don't know why you even bother to defend him.'

'You're right,' agreed Arianne. 'He's an idiot.'

'I wish you would stop sighing,' snapped Elodie when they sat together at the kitchen table. 'Your aunt tells me

67

you had an argument with the Belleville boy. You should either apologise or forget about it. It's no good moping.'

Elodie was ruthless about the memorial service for Luc's father.

'I promised Teresa we would all go.'

'But I don't go to church!'

'This is different.'

'Father never goes.'

'And look what happened to him!'

'What, would God have saved him from the Nazis if he'd been a Christian?'

'I promised.'

They arrived early for the service and sat a few rows back from the front. Arianne watched people stream into the church. There was no mistaking the current of excitement in the air. *Something* had brought them, though she wasn't convinced it was the memory of Luc's father. The past winter had been cold and hungry. Perhaps this memorial service was their way of giving thanks that it was over and they were still here. Her mind wandered. Cattle were lowing in the lane outside. She knew without seeing them that the Legros' farmhand was bringing them in for milking, could almost smell the farmyard on them, rising from their caramel hides. The evening sun caught the stained-glass windows of the nave, dotting the stone floor with pools of colour.

A murmur ran through the congregation. Teresa Belleville, very thin in a dark pre-war dress was walking down the aisle on the arm of her son, incongruous in a suit too tight across his shoulders. Father Julien walked behind them, his spectacles giving his round face the look of a surprised baby owl. Arianne stifled a giggle. Paul looked up hopefully. Elodie rapped each of them on the shoulder.

The service began.

'Jacques Belleville,' intoned Father Julien, 'was not a churchgoing man. Yet all of us who knew his paintings could tell that God had touched him with His grace.'

*God had touched him with His grace.* She liked the phrase. Grace. It occurred to her that this moment was full of it and she felt suddenly overwhelmed with affection – for Father Julien, for this building, for the villagers in their Sunday best. For Luc too, though it wasn't the same sort of affection. Her mind drifted to the world outside and she thought with unusual fondness of quiet Samaroux, mellowed by the centuries into an extension of the countryside so that one could never imagine that once it had not existed. This too, surely, was a form of grace. Despite everything, it seemed to Arianne, in this laden moment, that the world was as it should be.

'Is this what it means to believe in God?' she

wondered. It seemed unlikely that faith should be so easily stumbled upon.

The eulogy had ended and Father Julien had moved on to the mass. The invitation to communion was issued. Arianne shuffled down the aisle after Elodie.

Head bowed by the sacristy, she could not resist stealing a look at Luc. His eyes widened at the sight of her. *I was wrong about that suit*, she thought. *It's not too tight on him at all.*

Father Julien was saying something.

'I beg your pardon?' she said.

'I said, the Body of Christ.' Father Julien gazed at her over the top of his spectacles with an expression of mild rebuke. Arianne flushed.

'Amen?'

Father Julien sighed.

How was it possible to feel so much one minute and nothing the next? Arianne stood on the church steps after the service, watching Luc and his mother shake hands with their crowd of well-wishers. He had not spoken to her. Apart from that one quick glance in the church, he had not even looked at her.

'Dear God,' she prayed, 'please make that good feeling come back. Please let me be nice. Please, also, tell me what I should do.'

'You look troubled.' She started. Father Julien had appeared by her side and was looking at her with a benevolent smile.

'I was trying to pray.'

'Do I take it you were not succeeding?'

'I have no idea,' she admitted. 'I haven't really had much practice.'

'Do you feel, perhaps, that you would like guidance in this matter? Prayer, after all, is something of a speciality of mine.'

His blue eyes twinkled at her from behind his glasses.

'I think that would be lovely.' An idea struck her. 'Could I come to confession?'

'My child, what *have* you been up to?'

'I mean now?'

'Madame Belleville has invited me to her house to toast the memory of her husband.' Father Julien leaned forward to whisper. 'I understand she has unearthed champagne, and that Gaspard Félix has swapped a duck pâté for an old painting of her late husband's.'

'Gaspard Félix the butcher?'

'Do you know any other?'

'I didn't know he liked art.'

'People are forever surprising us. Now, about this confession.'

'I'm sure it won't take long.'

❧

'What do I do?' she asked minutes later in the confessional box.

'Tradition dictates that you ask me to forgive you and tell me when you last came to confession. Since that date is lost to the mists of time, I suggest you launch straight in and tell me what is troubling you.'

'I'm not sure I believe in God,' she warned him. 'Earlier, during the service, I thought I was brimming with faith, but then I went outside and it just vanished.'

'This can happen.' Father Julien settled himself on his narrow seat and closed his eyes. 'I'm listening.'

'It's not as if I've really *done* anything...'

'You'd be surprised what brings people to confession,' he said. 'Some thoughts, perhaps. Sad, angry thoughts?'

'I feel...' Like crying, she wanted to say. Like believing, in God, in Luc, in something. 'I want something to change.'

'Something?'

'Anything.'

'It's not so uncommon for the young to feel hemmed in. It is not a sin. It's even necessary, otherwise how would you ever get on?'

'But what can I *do* about it?'

'The world is big, Arianne. One day you will learn that each of us holds its image in our hearts. We are all mirrors of God, beings of infinite possibilities, and it is not necessary to look so very far afield to make new discoveries about the world or to understand our place in it. Study, prayer, the pleasures of simple things . . . these too can broaden and open our minds. Personally I believe they are the only paths to true wisdom. But the young are not interested in wisdom.'

'I'm not *un*interested,' said Arianne.

'Then I recommend patience until you finish school, and after that . . . travel, more study! The Germans have not closed the universities. Go to Bordeaux, as your mother did. Or Paris, why not? You are quite capable of it.'

'I would like to travel. Sometimes Samaroux feels so *small . . .*'

'Was there anything else? Only this champagne . . .'

'Why sometimes do people behave like you're really important to them and then refuse to talk to you because of a stupid argument?'

'Do I take it you are talking about young Luc?'

'Did *you* know about his grandfather?'

'What I know about my parishioners is really none of your concern.'

'I think he must think I mind. But I don't know if he minds thinking I think that. Which I don't. Mind, I mean. How did you know?'

The grille between them threw latticed shadows over his face, but she saw that he looked pained. 'Know what?' he asked.

'You know . . . Luc,' she hissed. 'Is it that obvious?'

'Arianne, my dear, you hardly took your eyes off him throughout the service.'

'That's not true!'

'I'll be the judge of that.'

Arianne waited in silence for the heat in her cheeks to die down.

'What should I do?' she asked at last.

'I am a priest, not a relationship counsellor. It does strike me that if you love this boy, perhaps the simplest thing to do would be to tell him so?'

'I don't *love* him! I just wish I knew where I stand. We were friends.'

'Do you not see in his treatment of you a reflection of your treatment of God?'

'God! What does God have to do with anything?'

'*Earlier I was brimming with faith, but as soon as I came out it just vanished.* You loved God and then you did not love God. You do not trust your feelings for God. Some relationships are more difficult to apprehend than others. They are usually the more meaningful ones.'

'You mean . . .'

'Dear Arianne. Would it help if I said that you are not the first soul-searching teenager who has come to me looking for answers?'

'Do you mean Luc? Has *he* been talking to you?'

Father Julien shifted behind his lattice screen. 'Faith and love, child. There is nothing more important. Now, I think we have reached the end of this confession. We must not keep the widow Belleville waiting a moment longer.'

'We?'

'I am taking you with me,' he announced, 'as my guest.'

'But...'

'But what?'

'Shouldn't you absolve me first?'

'I absolve you.' The old priest made an approximate sign of the cross as he climbed out of the confessional box. 'Come along.'

'You're not a normal priest.'

'How would you know?' He was already halfway down the aisle before she hurried after him.

IV

Solange collared Luc by the kitchen door when his mother sent him to fetch more wine.

'I'm not going to pretend I don't know what it's all about,' she said. 'Because I do.'

'I have no idea what you're talking about.'

'Ari. I know why you quarrelled, and I'm sorry to

bring it up at your father's memorial and everything, but I think you've behaved like an absolute thug.'

Madame Jarvis, emerging from the kitchen, raised her eyebrows. Solange glared at her and she scurried away.

Luc's eyes flashed as he glanced around the room. 'It's none of your business.'

'She's my cousin.'

'You have no idea what we've been through.'

'What *you've* been through? Funny, when I heard about what happened, I didn't think about *you* at all. I thought about the family who were arrested because of your grandfather, and I thought of my poor cousin sobbing away in bed at night because *somebody* is too bloody stubborn to realise she would never in a million years give away his secret.'

'She told *you*.'

'Only because I beat it out of her, because she was so upset. He's a creep, I said, but she *would* defend you. For God's sake, this is the girl who talked to *nobody at all* for almost a year when her father was taken prisoner.'

'Except her brother.'

'Ah,' said Solange. 'Her brother.'

'There you are!' Teresa Belleville descended on them a few minutes later. 'Whatever are you whispering about? Luc, *chéri,* Father Julien has just arrived, so we can open the champagne. I'm going to fetch the pâté, so could you go and offer him a drink? There's somebody with him – oh, Solange, it's your cousin. I wonder why she didn't come with your great-aunt.'

'I really don't know why she ever thought this party was a good idea,' said Luc when she had gone. 'She's been having kittens all week.'

'You heard what your mama said, *chéri*,' said Solange. 'Go and offer the man a drink.'

❧

Arianne wouldn't look at him as he approached, but Father Julien beamed.

'Luc, my boy! Just the man we were looking for. With bubbles! Arianne here has just been to confession. I'm sure she'd love to tell you all about it.'

Arianne glowered. Father Julien's beam grew wider.

'Pour it out then, my boy!'

Luc poured. Father Julien stuck his nose into the glass, heaved a sigh of satisfaction and bustled off, taking the bottle with him.

'There's Sol,' said Arianne. She waved, but Solange turned away.

A tendril of hair had fallen over her face. She raised a hand to push it back, and he was distracted by the way the gesture caused her breasts to rise in her dark slim-fitting dress.

'It wasn't a real confession,' she said. 'More like a chat.'

Her voice was very low. He leant in closer to close out the noise of the room.

'What did you chat about?'

'Oh, you know.' She waved her hand. 'God things.'

Their heads were almost touching. He swallowed. She smelt of jasmine.

'Look,' he began.

'I just want . . .'

They broke off at the same time.

'You go,' she said.

'No, you first.'

She looked around the room as if she were only just taking it in.

'I can't do this,' he thought he heard. He braced himself for whatever she had to say, then froze when she stepped forward to take his hands in hers.

Her skin against his was soft. He closed his eyes and felt her lips brush his cheek.

'I'm sorry,' she murmured. And then, before he could react, she was gone.

V

He would have followed her at once, but his mother protested.

'Better wait,' said Solange. 'I'll tell you exactly what to do.'

He had never stopped to look at the old holm oak by her house before, but it was exactly as Solange had described it, growing right on the boundary of the property. Arianne's father had refused to cut it down and over the years the garden wall had been rebuilt to incorporate it. Its lowest branch was within easy reach of the street. He grasped it and swung himself up.

'Beneath the wall is the old dog pen. Don't jump, or you'll never get back up again, and the only way out is through the garden at the back – they lost the key to the door in the wall ages ago, though to be honest even Paul could kick it down. You have to climb from the wall on to the roof. Ari's window is right at the end. It's a bit slippery, but you should be all right, we've done it loads of times. She doesn't have shutters up there.'

'I'll give her the shock of her life.'

'She'll love it.'

∽∾

'You're not *much* of a burglar.'

His heart skipped a beat at the sound of her voice. He looked up to where she sat cross-legged on a flat ledge between two chimney stacks, the red glow of a cigarette between her fingers.

'The racket you're making!' she said. 'What on earth are you doing?'

'I came to see you.'

'Well, you've seen me now, so you'd better go.'

He hoisted himself up to where she was sitting.

'I meant it,' she protested. 'My life won't be worth living if Auntie Elodie hears you.'

'I didn't know you smoked.'

'There's a lot you don't know about me.' She didn't inhale, he noticed. She saw him smile, took a more robust drag and broke into a cough.

'Come.' He stubbed the cigarette out against a tile and flicked it into the street below. 'I've got something to show you.'

'What?'

'Trust me.' He slithered down the roof back to the tree and grabbed a branch with both hands.

'It's past curfew,' she said.

'I promise we won't get caught.'

She edged towards the tree.

'Tell me where we're going first,' she whispered. 'Or I won't come.'

'Jump!' He opened his arms. 'I want to show you something.'

Her hand in his, stifling laughter, they ran through the sleeping village.

'This is crazy!'

'Shh, keep your voice down!'

On they ran past the village houses, along the low wall

of the cemetery, past its gates and the shadows of crosses, up the lane which snaked through the woods towards the main road to Limoges.

'I don't know when I last came up here.' Arianne was still whispering, though they had left the last chalet behind. 'I always stop at the cemetery.'

'How often do you go?'

'Every Friday. Papa used to take her flowers.'

He turned to look at her, but she didn't look sad.

'And now it's your turn,' he said.

She smiled. 'And now it's my turn.'

Away from the village, in a world drained of colour, the road stretched before them like a silver ribbon and the sounds of the night rang across the countryside with the clarity of church bells. An owl screeched. Its victim screamed. A brook rushed in the distance. They stopped by a gate at the top of the hill.

'We go this way,' said Luc.

Arianne paused as she climbed over the gate, standing astride it to survey her surroundings. Behind them lay Samaroux and open country. Ahead, branches of oak and beech arched over a path, forming a tunnel which stretched into the woods.

'There ought to be wolves,' she said. 'Or talking bears.'

'Unlikely in these parts. We could probably stretch to a wild boar . . .'

'You know what I mean though?'

'Of course I do.' He held out his hand. 'Come.'

She stopped again after a few steps to breathe in the damp air. 'I don't think I've ever heard such silence,' she said. 'Or felt so utterly alone.'

'We have to hurry.'

'*Why* won't you tell me where we're going?'

'It's a surprise.'

'I can see,' she remarked. 'Almost clearly.'

Luc grunted.

'Is it night vision?'

'No.' The trees were thinning out now. He stood to one side to let her continue alone. 'It's the moon.'

'Oh,' breathed Arianne.

The moon indeed. His peace offering, full and low, caught in the arch of the trees at the end of the tunnel. It shimmered over the valley, its seas and craters stark against its ripe, round shape.

'How small we are,' said Arianne at last. 'And how beautiful it is.'

'Soon it will rise higher,' said Luc. 'And lose the effect of the trees.'

'I could almost *touch* it.'

'That's how I felt the first time I saw it.'

'Do you often wander around at night?'

'Lately, yes.'

He had been crouching on his heels and now let himself fall back on the grass with his back against a tree. Arianne sat beside him. The moon shook itself free of the trees and floated untethered in the inky sky.

'It's like there are two worlds,' he said at last. 'There's the real one, the messy one, with school and Grandfather and the Occupation. And there's this one, where everything seems to be just right. Like time's been suspended, and life and death and happiness and sadness are all part of the same thing. It makes me feel that this is how things were always meant to be. Beauty and cruelty. Here in the world of wolves and moons and talking bears. Does that make sense?'

'Parts of it. Which world do I belong to?'

'I don't know.'

She leaned forward and touched two fingers to his lips.

'I'm very real,' she said.

He groaned and pulled her into his arms.

She lay against him on a bed of dew-soaked grass. Neither of them noticed the dampness which seeped through their clothes and soaked their skin, or the cold air on their limbs. There was only his mouth on hers, the softness of her body against his, her hands winding round the back of his neck, drawing him closer. She bit his lip and wrapped her legs around his. He broke away to lie on his back, pulling her with him so that her head rested in the crook of his shoulder.

'Stars,' he said. 'In the sky, I mean. As well as in my head.'

'Told you I was real.'

'I'm still not completely convinced.'

❧

The sky was streaked with red by the time they returned to the village.

'They won't have missed you?' he whispered.

'I shouldn't think so. You?'

'Doubt it. Mother goes to bed early. And even if she does . . .' They had reached the wall of Arianne's garden. She stood with her back to it, his hands against the stone on either side of her. She hooked her fingers into his belt.

'What?' she murmured.

'It's worth it,' he whispered back.

The church bells chimed. The village was beginning to stir.

'Help me up?'

He linked his hands together to give her a leg up and she pulled herself on to the wall.

'Good night, Romeo,' she grinned.

She stood on the roof of her parents' house, a slight silhouette against the pink and indigo of morning, as unreal and wonderful to him in that moment as the happiness rising within him.

'You'll fall,' he warned.

She laughed. He caught glimpses of her thighs as she crawled over the tiles. She turned to look back at him. A strand of hair caught in her mouth and he itched to push it aside.

'Luc?'

'What?'

Somewhere in the countryside, another church bell rang. Arianne smiled

'It's Sunday morning,' she said.

He felt like he had wings, running home on the dirt pavement as if he were cutting through air. Arianne knelt for a while by her open window, gazing without seeing it at the morning sky. Then she crawled towards her bed and slept.

# May 1944

I

Samaroux was delighted to have a new source of gossip.

'So,' teased Thierry in the Café de la Paix. 'The Lafayette wench.'

'All the girls are madly jealous,' Solange told Arianne on their way into a geography class. 'But most of the boys don't get it.'

'I suppose I'll see even less of you now,' Teresa complained to Luc.

'Don't think for a minute you can let up on your schoolwork,' threatened Elodie.

Luc hated the gossip but Arianne didn't care.

'I feel like a different person,' she confided in Solange. 'Incandescent. Lit up. Happy.'

'Like someone has lifted the lid on your emotions and they are all just bubbling up to the surface?' asked Solange.

'Yes!' cried Arianne. 'Exactly like that! How did you know?'

'I read about it in one of Maman's magazines,' said Solange drily.

But Luc was approaching and Arianne wasn't listening.

'Look at him,' she sighed. 'Isn't he lovely?'

It wasn't possible to be really jealous of Arianne, thought Solange. Not if you loved her. Her happiness was too infectious. She went with them to Lascande that afternoon, and lay beside them on the lawn.

'We won't be like other people.' Luc pointed a finger at the sky, tracing their destiny. 'None of us. We will all be different.'

'Oh really?' laughed Solange.

'How?' asked Arianne.

'We shan't stay here for a start. We'll travel all over the world. We'll go everywhere, and when we're bored we'll just move on somewhere else.'

'We'll have pots of money,' cried Arianne. 'Left to us by long-lost millionaire uncles. We'll go to Venice and have a huge motorboat and live in a palace.'

'And then to New York where we'll live in a sky-scraper.'

'We'll have a castle in Hungary . . .'

'A yacht in the Caribbean and an igloo in Alaska . . .'

'An igloo!'

'You think we'd be cold, but we wouldn't. We'd have

sleeping bags lined with fur, and a fire, and we'd rub each other's skin with whale fat to stop us getting frostbite.'

'Excuse me?' interjected Solange. 'Am I part of the whale-fat rubbing, or is this a private fantasy?'

Luc blew her a kiss. Arianne laughed. Sol smiled and tilted her face towards the sun. It was the first truly hot day of the year, and the sky through their narrowed eyes was the colour of amethysts. Swallows flew high, too high to make out their cries, but they felt their hearts soar with them.

'I don't think I have ever felt happier than at this moment,' said Arianne, but even as she said it Solange could tell that the moment had passed. Arianne rolled back over to Luc, sitting right up against him with her arms around his waist and her face pressed into his shirt.

'I don't have a long-lost uncle,' she said.

'You don't *know* that,' he murmured. 'That's the whole point of him being lost.'

'We'll have to take Paul with us. We can't leave him with Auntie Elodie, no matter how annoying he is.'

'He can have his own yacht,' said Luc. 'And Sol too, of course.'

'Thanks.' Solange smiled.

'Do you really think we'll be able to?' asked Arianne. Luc was nuzzling her neck and she had to push him away to speak. 'Not the yacht, I mean, but travel and go where we want and see the world?'

''Course we can. When the Germans leave.'

'*If* they leave.'

'They will. It'll be over soon.'

'People keep saying that but how can they possibly know?'

'It's all over the BBC.'

'When do you listen to the BBC?'

Luc shifted guiltily.

'When?' she repeated.

'Thierry has a radio in his barn.'

'I didn't know that.' Arianne turned to Solange. 'Did you know that?'

Solange shrugged. 'Put it this way, I'm not blinded by love.'

'But it's dangerous!'

'Not so very.' Luc pulled her back to him and trailed his lips along her collarbone.

'I'm still here?' said Solange.

'Promise you won't listen to it again,' said Arianne.

Luc's lips moved to her earlobe.

'I'm going home,' said Solange

They barely noticed her leave. She turned back when she reached the path. The house crouched on the edge of the lawn, hugged by the forest which hid it from Samaroux. Luc and Arianne had moved to the terrace. She sat beside him on the wall with her head on his shoulder, looking out across the countryside to where the rolling green of the hills faded to a haze of blue. The low evening sun cast its shadows around them but to Solange the boy and girl on the terrace *shimmered* in the evening light. In that moment before she turned for home, they looked like ghosts, ghosts who had always been there and who always would be.

No, she wasn't jealous. They were just too perfect.

## II

Sevastopol fell in the middle of May. The remains of the German Seventeenth Army in the Crimea were destroyed shortly afterwards, and 36,000 Axis troops taken prisoner. The Russians were turning now to Belorussia, and the Allies were preparing their invasion from the west.

Spring had been and gone. Soon the heat would return, and with it mosquitoes and disease. Captain Drechsler's men had shed their greatcoats and were restless. They knew they were losing the war. When the end came, they wanted to be near home.

In the middle of May their wish came true. The Captain swept into the barn where they took their meals, brandishing a telegram. He'd been drinking, but they knew that this was something different. The flush was back in his cheek and the sparkle in his eye. He looked young again, and handsome.

'Gather your kit, men!' he shouted. 'All hands on deck and at the double! We're on our way back to the Fatherland.'

'Home, Alois,' sighed the Captain later that evening. 'Your wife and little boy. My parents, my music. Good beer, good wine. No more of this god-awful vodka.'

Alois Grand lit a cigarette. 'Going straight back, are we?' he asked.

'Small redeployment in France first,' admitted the Captain.

'To fight the Americans.'

'If they land.'

'They'll land. Stubborn sods, the Americans.'

'Still,' said the Captain cheerfully. 'It'll be good to do some proper fighting again, eh?'

Alois exhaled a series of perfect smoke rings. 'Between you and me, sir,' he said, 'I'd much rather go home.'


### III

Romy sat at the terrace of the Café de la Paix after lunch one Sunday, an unopened book in his hand, gazing towards Arianne's front door and dreaming about buying Lascande.

He knew she loved the place. He had followed her there several times, and Paul had told him about her childhood visit with her mother. He had no idea how he was going to buy it, but he knew just how things would be once he had it. They would all live there together. His mother would be happy and keep house, and Arianne's fearsome great-aunt would be somehow neutralised and kept in a rocking chair, and his father would have vaporised – he couldn't quite bring himself to dream that he was dead. Arianne would sit at his feet and listen as he read out loud from his favourite books. He would play the piano for her while she sang, they would walk together in the woods and she would let him hold her hand.

'We never even write to Papa any more,' Paul had grumbled to him earlier that week. 'That was two things you could always rely on with Arianne. Fridays she went to the cemetery, and Sundays we wrote to Papa. I could turn into Heil Hitler and she wouldn't even notice. It'll be the same again this Sunday, see if it isn't. I mean I don't *care*, obviously. It's not like I *enjoy* writing letters. But still.'

Sure enough, Arianne and Luc were emerging from her house. Romy threw a few coins on the table and followed at a discreet distance. They took the road out of the village and turned right when they reached the woods. Not Lascande today, then. They walked on past the old fountain and followed the brook upstream to where it widened into a pool. It was not yet late enough in the year for the sun to warm the air beneath the trees. The water was deep, the clear surface fading to amber and then to brown in the depths, reflecting the colour of the rocks. Leaves floated on the surface. Somewhere above, a cuckoo called. Romy crept closer.

'Swim,' Arianne was saying. 'Or don't you dare?'

'I don't see you getting in.'

Arianne took the bait and crossed the water upstream from where Luc stood. Facing him across the pool, she slipped her feet out of her wooden clogs. Romy squirmed. She raised her arms above her head to undo the catch of her dress, twisted them to grip the zipper. She tugged, faltered, then pulled the dress over her head. Romy caught his breath.

'Don't watch.'

She slipped into the pool.

'I did it,' she gasped.

'Twenty strokes or it doesn't count.'

He counted out loud as her flailing steadied. The pool was too small for anything but swimming in circles.

'I feel absurd,' she said.

'You can come out now.'

But Arianne did not come out. Instead she laughed and rolled on to her back.

'It's lovely after the initial shock.'

Luc growled something Romy could not hear. The current had carried her to the edge of the pool and was nudging her against the boulders. She hoisted herself into a puddle of sunshine and wrapped her arms around her legs. Her dark hair, raked back from her face, continued to drip water down her neck, and a stream of droplets flowed over her collarbone into the fabric of her sodden bra.

'The first time I saw you, you were in the water,' she said.

'Hardly the first time you saw me.'

'The first time I saw you properly.'

He lay on his side, looking at her. 'You were wearing a white dress with a green streak down the back from sitting in the grass.'

'You remember that?'

'I loved that green streak. It said so much about you.'

She shivered.

'Come here.' Luc's voice was thick and low.

'I'm not sure that's a good idea.'

'I only want to dry you.'

She picked up her clothes and went to him. He shrugged off his shirt and used it to dry her back, dropping kisses along her shoulder blades. She pushed him away without conviction.

Romy could take it no longer. He turned tail and ran, not caring if they heard him.

ൟ

'Someone's in a hurry.' Marie Dupont squinted into the sun which pierced the clearing where she sat with her sister and Paul mending their emptied snares. 'Who'd go crashing through the woods like that?'

'I'll go and see.' Her younger sister Charlotte skipped barefoot to the edge of the trees, then just as quickly skipped back. 'It's Romy!' she hissed.

'That loser!' sneered Paul.

'He's coming this way! And he's crying!'

'He's probably been spying on Ari again. He's so pathetic.'

'Does he still love her?' asked Marie.

'Yeah, and she hates him.'

'Poor Romy,' sighed Marie. 'I wish someone loved me like that.'

'Don't be such a girl.' Paul scowled.

Marie wore blue overalls and Paul's own hand-me-down boots, but her eyelashes were long and curly as they fluttered over her mud-streaked cheeks. Paul went pink and she giggled.

'I hate him,' said Charlotte. 'He was with his father last time he came for the money.'

'Let's go then,' said Paul.

They ran as fast as they could to get away from Romy, and then they ran some more for the sheer pleasure of it, chasing each other back and forth across the stream until they reached the village. They collapsed in a panting heap in Paul's garden and he drew water from the well for them to drink.

'I love it here,' said Marie, when they had drunk their fill.

'It's your home now,' said Paul.

The sisters exchanged glances.

'What?' said Paul.

'It's nothing.' Marie shook her head at her sister.

'*What*?' Paul flipped on to his stomach and looked from one sister to the other. 'You've got to tell me. I'm your friend.'

'I *want* to tell him,' whined Charlotte.

Marie bit her lip. Paul reached out and covered her small brown hand with his.

'All right.' She sighed. 'I'll tell you.'

∾

'But there must be a reason,' said Arianne later that evening. She, Luc and Solange stood in a concerned semi-circle around Paul, who sat with his back pressed against the well in the descending twilight. 'You never cry, *and* it's dinnertime.'

'I'm not allowed to say.' Paul wiped away his tears with the heel of his hand.

'Oh, you big baby.' Arianne knelt beside him and

pulled him into her arms. He burrowed his head into her shoulder. 'What could possibly be so bad?'

'Marie's leaving!' wailed Paul. He flung himself out of her arms and on to the ground.

'Paul's in love!' yelped Solange. 'Oh, *sweet*!'

'Shut up!' howled Paul.

'But where is she going?' asked Arianne. 'You'll see her again, darling. You can write to her, and visit . . .'

'Ari.' Luc's expression was sombre as he crouched beside her. 'Paul, mate. Do you want to tell us what happened?'

'I don't understand,' muttered Paul. 'Just she said their father didn't have any more money to pay Romy's dad, so he has to go.'

'Romy's dad?' Arianne wondered.

'Protection money,' said Luc.

'I don't understand either.'

'He's blackmailing them.'

'But why?'

'Oh, Ari.' Luc reached out and cupped her cheek in his hand. 'Don't say you hadn't guessed.'

'He means they're Jews,' said Solange.

'They're not!' yelled Paul.

'Yes, they are,' said Luc. He pulled Paul to his feet. 'And you, my friend, have got to promise not to tell another soul what you have just told us. Can you do that?

You have to be as brave and good as I know you can be and pretend you don't know a thing.'

Paul looked at Arianne. She nodded.

'I'm not crying,' he said.

'I know you're not.' She pulled him into another hug. 'When Papa comes home,' she whispered into his hair, 'I'm going to tell him how amazing you've been. Keeping us fed, all those rabbits and fish. He's going to be so proud of you.'

'You won't tell him about the bad stuff?'

'What bad stuff?' Arianne smiled.

'You know . . .'

She kissed the top of his head. 'I don't remember any bad stuff.'

Luc and Solange stayed for supper that night. Elodie grumbled but fetched an extra jar of preserved fruit from the larder. Solange ran home and returned with a freshly made goat's cheese, and Luc brought wine which Arianne mixed with water for Paul. Elodie went to bed early but the others talked late into the night, with Solange in an armchair and Luc on the floor by the sofa where a sleepy Paul lay with his head on his sister's lap.

'I'm glad you're not cross with me any more.' Paul yawned.

'So am I,' said Arianne.

Luc reached out behind him and took her hand.

'I haven't felt like this for ages,' he murmured.

'Like what?' asked Solange.

She was surprised by the gentleness of his smile.

'Like a family,' he answered.

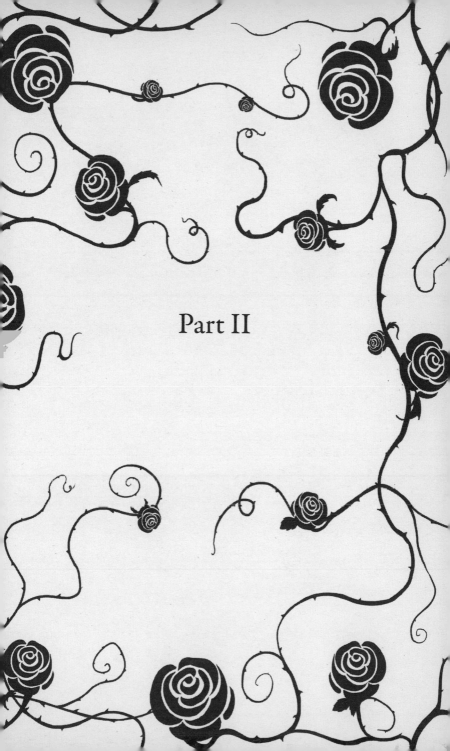

Part II

# June 6th, 1944

*The Duponts didn't leave immediately but we forgot about them soon enough in the light of what was going on in the north. News trickled down the secret information network from the BBC in London to the forbidden radio in Thierry Legros's barn. Word spread, whispered at first, then more confident. The Allies had landed in Normandy!*

*In my mind's eye, I have a picture of how it happened.*

*I see the ocean, the dark light which precedes dawn. The night shaking with the roar of aircraft crossing the sea which separates Europe from England, 500 kilometres north of Samaroux. Pale figures dropping from the planes, silk mushrooming above them, slowing their descent as they fall through darkness to land on beaches, in fields, in the sea itself. Some are hurt. Some drown. Most survive to fight.*

*Under a clouded moon, the beaches gleam. Cotentin, Caen, Orne, Odon, Falaise, minerals and particles of rock, ground to sand by the pounding of waves. They have new names today, in a new language. Gold, Juno, Omaha,*

Utah, Sword. In the pearl and grey of morning, flat-bottomed landing craft struggle to the coast, belching men into the sea. They stagger through the ebb and pull of the water, the relentless undertow. The guns awake in the fortified dunes. Shells hit the water and the tottering men are blown sideways, blown to pieces, blown under, but still the craft keep coming while the skies above them thunder.

I see the bodies of the dead and the debris of war strewn across the sand.

The Allies are back. The tide of war is turning.

And the waves continue to pound the shore, washing over particles of rock.

# June 7th, 1944

Luc finished school before Arianne that Wednesday but he didn't wait. She found him when she came back from the station with Solange, drinking at a crowded table outside the Café de la Paix.

'Ari! Sol!' He threw an arm around Arianne's waist. 'Have a drink!' He poured out two glasses of wine. Several men cheered. Someone shouted, 'To the Americans!' Someone else punched him and told him to keep his trap shut.

'What are we drinking to?' asked Arianne.

Luc motioned them closer, sliding his hands over their backs until their heads were touching. 'It's started,' he whispered.

'What's started?' Solange giggled as Thierry pulled her on to his lap.

'The liberation, donkey, what d'you think? The Americans landed in Normandy yesterday.'

'And the English,' hiccupped Thierry.

'*To the English*', someone called, and they emptied their glasses.

'Come with me to Lascande,' whispered Luc in Arianne's ear.

'There isn't time before supper.'

'To the woods, then. To the pool for a swim.' His hand crept around her waist, inching towards her breast.

'Too cold.' She pushed him away, laughing, aware of people watching.

'*To women!*' someone shouted, and they drank again.

A car crawled past and stopped a few doors down from the café. Four men in Milice uniform got out. The laughter in the café stopped.

'What the hell are they doing here?' asked Jérôme.

'Hide the bottle, quick!'

'We're allowed to drink, aren't we?'

Luc pushed Arianne away and stood up slowly.

'They've come for the Duponts,' said Luc.

'You don't know that,' whispered Arianne.

'Yes, I do. I know that's what they're doing.'

They stood and shuffled round the table to the street.

A small crowd had already gathered outside the Duponts' house. From the back, Arianne caught only glimpses – the blue of Miliciens' uniforms, a gun raised like a truncheon, a wide-open front door. Mayor Jarvis stood by the car, hands pressed together, face drawn.

'I thought they always came at night.' Odile Jouvert, the baker's wife, stood on tiptoe to get a better view.

'Not any more,' said her husband.

Joseph Dupont stumbled out of the house, followed by his wife and daughters. He stopped when he saw the crowd gathered outside. One of the Miliciens drove his rifle butt into his ribs. He groaned. Charlotte howled. The car doors slammed shut behind them and the engine roared.

Another small figure burst out of the house, blazing copper hair standing on end, his half-open school bag still slung across his body trailing books and papers.

'Stop!' screamed Paul. 'Somebody, stop them!'

'Oh my God,' breathed Arianne. 'Paul was with them.'

She broke away from Luc and began to run towards her brother, shouting for him as she clawed her way through the crowd.

'Ari. It's all right. Don't cry, it's all right.'

Romy had appeared beside her. He took her arm and began to clear a passage through the throng.

'You!' Luc was also at her side, incandescent with rage. He barrelled into Romy, knocked him to the ground and raised his fist.

'Enough!' Father Julien stepped out of the crowd and seized Luc by the arm.

'I'll kill him!' yelled Luc.

'Quiet!' Father Julien was stronger than he looked. Luc, pinned to his chest, quivered with anger. 'Romy, are you all right?' Romy nodded and scrambled to his feet.

'Go home to your mother. You, boy,' he barked at Luc. 'Come with me.'

ᔊᓍ

'I have to go and see Luc,' Arianne told Elodie later that evening.

'Is your brother asleep?'

'He's out cold. I gave him some more wine and water.'

'He'll be developing a taste for it if you're not careful.'

Arianne hesitated on the front step, then turned back towards her great-aunt.

'Apart from finding Maman when she died,' she said, 'I think today was the worst thing I ever saw.'

'Yes,' said Elodie. 'I think it probably was.'

'For you too?'

'I've seen other wars.'

'They won't come back, will they? The Duponts, I mean.'

'No, child,' murmured Elodie. 'They won't come back.'

Still Arianne lingered, looking out into the twilit street.

'Go,' said Elodie. 'Just make sure you're back before curfew.'

She found his mother alone in her kitchen, a bottle of eau de vie and two glasses on the table.

'He's in his room,' slurred Teresa. 'You can go up if you like. Try to make him see sense. I won't chaperone you.'

All this time and she had never seen his room! She was struck by how bare it was. A bed, a chest of drawers, a table and chair. Schoolbooks but no novels, nothing to mark it out as his. He sat on the window ledge and did not get up when he saw her.

'I came to see if you were all right.'

'Come here.'

His breath tasted of alcohol. She turned her face away. His hand closed around her waist, and he pulled her roughly towards him.

'If it weren't for you,' he whispered against her mouth.

'You're hurting me . . .'

He cupped her face in his hands and pressed his forehead to hers. 'You're beautiful,' he mumbled. 'But I have to do something. I can't just sit around and wait.'

'What are you talking about?' But Luc had passed out, his head on her shoulder. She dragged him off the window seat to the bed, pulled the blankets over him and went downstairs.

'How is he?' asked his mother.

'Out. Angry. Maudlin. I've never seen him drunk before.'

'We've both had a shock.' Elbows resting on the table,

Teresa pressed the heels of her hands into her eyes. 'I hoped it would be different here.'

'It's never happened before. People being taken, I mean. Not from the actual village. Not like that, in broad *daylight*.'

'But it's happening now. We'll lose him, Arianne. See if we don't.'

'Lose him?'

'They'll all go. All the young men. Fighting with the Americans. I hate the bloody Americans!'

'Luc won't go. He . . .'

*I have to do something.*

'What?' Teresa drained the last drops from her glass. 'You think he'll stay for you?'

Arianne tilted her chin.

*I can't just sit around and wait.*

'He'll forget about us.' Teresa started to cry. 'He'll forget he even had a mother . . .'

'You mustn't say that!' Arianne patted the older woman on the arm. 'He loves you, he's always telling me so.'

'Liar,' sniffed Teresa.

'I'll send my aunt to see you in the morning.' Arianne began to edge towards the door. Teresa's crying turned to sobs.

'Make him stay!' she wailed. 'You're a woman now, Arianne. Don't let him get away!'

# June 8th, 1944

Her schoolbag was not big enough for everything she needed, but to go out carrying anything else would raise Elodie's suspicions. She had raided the larder in the night. A jar of cherries in eau de vie, a fresh goat's cheese, Elodie's emergency chocolate. She would get into trouble afterwards, but it couldn't be helped. She saved her bread from breakfast, smuggling it up to her room to pack with the other things she wanted – candles, matches, a pair of sheets.

She wove her hair into a plait and checked her appearance in the mirror. No extra flush, no hint of dissipation gave her away. Elodie, when she bade her goodbye, did not notice anything amiss. She had worried Luc might not be at the station, but he was there as usual, not looking very much the worse for yesterday's excesses.

'I'm sorry,' he said as soon as he saw her. 'For anything I did or said. I'm sorry, I'm sorry, I'm sorry.'

'You were upset. It was a terrible day.' She lowered her voice as she had heard film actresses do, hoping she was not ridiculous. 'Meet me at Lascande at midday,' she murmured.

'What?'

'Midday, mind,' she breathed. 'Not before.'

֎

*I am mad,* she thought as she sped through the woods. After all the lectures she had given Paul, to be cutting school herself! Her father's last words to her, almost, *be good, study hard, do your mother proud*, and yet here she was, out on a school day, skipping a geography test! The birdsong today was deafening, the morning light hard and clear, the ground damp with dew. Arianne had started at a run but slowed to an amble by the time she reached the faded signpost, and it seemed to her that this sharpening of the senses, this being in tune with her surroundings were as much a part of her preparations as all she had done and all she had yet to do.

She let herself into the house and set to work at once in the bedroom. She threw open windows and swept the floor, she dusted the furniture. She went out to the garden and picked some early roses, she laid out her stolen food. She shook the bedspread out on the lawn, and washed herself in the giant's bathtub. She took the linen sheets out of her school bag and made the bed.

He came at twelve as she had asked him to, and followed a trail of rose petals from the scullery door to the four-poster bedroom where she waited for him with her hair brushed out, in an old satin nightgown of her mother's. *A woman*, his mother had said, but she felt like a little girl.

'Ari,' he murmured, and closed the door behind him.

∞

'I love you,' she whispered afterwards. He smiled and she thought, *I have never seen that smile before.* He pulled her close and they lay skin to skin and mouth to mouth with all their limbs entangled.

'I love you too,' he whispered back.

*He'll never leave now*, thought Arianne.

The light outside mellowed into afternoon. The room grew quiet and they slept.

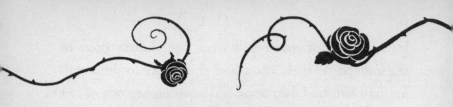

# June 9th, 1944

## I

Solange lay in wait for her on the road to school and wheedled out the truth before they even reached the station.

'You didn't! Before me! You can't have!'

'Shush, Sol, people are watching . . .'

'But was it nice?'

'Yes.' She smiled. 'It was nice.'

Luc and Arianne did not touch that morning on the way to school but stood a foot away from each other in the train carriage, not even speaking. Her cheeks flamed when she met his eye. He smiled, and for a moment she hoped he was going to pull her to him right there, in front of all the commuters; she wanted to feel his arms around her again, his mouth in her hair, his voice telling her over and over that he loved her . . .

'I can't wait this afternoon,' he told her as they parted at the school gate. 'But I'll come round this evening. Leave your window open?'

'*Leave your window open . . .*' sighed Solange as he walked off.

'Shut *up*,' hissed Arianne.

All day, she hugged her secret close. Luc Belleville loved her. Luc Belleville was her lover. Luc Belleville was hers, in every way. Lunchtime came and went, afternoon and evening. At last, when Paul and Elodie were asleep, she climbed out of her bedroom window on to the roof.

He was already waiting in the shadows, a bunch of wild carnations in his hand, but his kiss was fleeting.

'Come,' he said. 'Let's walk.'

He took her by the hand and led her past the cemetery, up the ribbon of road and into the woods to the place they had first kissed. And there, under a moon which tonight was no more than a sliver, he told her he was leaving.

∽

'But you can't leave! Yesterday . . . You can't just leave like it doesn't matter!'

She sat cross-legged on the ground before him, her hands clutching the flowers in her lap.

'Of course it matters. That's why I have to go.'

'But that doesn't make sense!'

'I want you to be proud.'

'*Proud*?' A memory came to her, walking out with

Luc the morning after their first kiss, down towards the stream, leaning in towards each other, pretending not to see their peers stare, unable not to grin. She clasped his hands and pressed her lips to them.

'I want you to be proud of me,' he repeated.

She dropped his hands, feeling defeated.

'I heard the Maquis were starving,' she said. 'And I heard you can expect to last three months in the Résistance.'

'Father Julien says the war will be over before then.'

'What does he have to do with it?'

Luc did not answer.

'Tell me!' she insisted. 'You have to tell me! When you're killed, I want to know, I need to know, why . . .' Her voice broke. She buried her face in her knees.

'He's the leader.' Luc sighed. 'All the Résistance activity around here, he coordinates it. He's been going for years, right under Romy's father's nose.'

'*Father Julien?*'

'Who'd have thought, eh? So it's not true you only last three months. And you're not supposed to know.'

'But what do you have to do?'

He would not look at her. 'Tell me!' she ordered. He sighed.

'Two men. I have to meet them tonight and hide them, then lead them to another safe house tomorrow. I'm only telling you because after that I'm not coming back. I'm going with them when they leave. Father Julien doesn't know that bit.'

'Who are they?'

'They're not from around here.'

'Where are you meeting them?'

'I can't tell you that.'

'Oh, for God's sake! Where are you hiding them, then?'

He looked away.

'Not Lascande,' she cried. 'You can't!'

'He's used it before.' He still wouldn't look at her. 'You know the first time we went and you thought someone had been there?'

'But you *can't* . . .'

'It's only for one day. We'll be off again by nightfall tomorrow.'

'Off . . .'

'Think of your father. *He* went off to fight. *He* was brave.'

'But look what happened to him!'

'Ari, be reasonable! It's about more than us, now, can't you see? I love you, of course I do, but some things . . . some things just have to be done.'

'Father Julien once told me there was *nothing* more important than love.'

'I didn't say love wasn't important.'

'You meant it though. Love is less important than

running around pretending to be a soldier, pretending you can make a difference.'

'We *will* make a difference.'

'But you're *sixteen*. You're a *child*.'

'Ari . . .' He took her hand. 'We're not children,' he whispered against her mouth.

She pushed him away and scrambled to her feet.

'Goodbye, Luc. I don't suppose I'll ever see you again. Seeing as you're obviously about to get *killed*.'

She picked up her cardigan and her bunch of wild carnations. She thought of throwing them in his face then reflected bitterly that these were all she had left of him. They turned for home. She blinked back tears as they passed the cemetery. He tried to take her hand but she shook him off.

'Come to Lascande tomorrow,' he begged when they reached the holm oak. 'Please? We can go together after school.'

'*School*?'

'Father Julien says tomorrow has to be completely normal. I have to be back before dawn. We don't leave again until after nightfall.'

'What, so you want me to come with you so you can *screw* me with your friends watching?'

He looked shocked. Arianne laid out her terms.

'If you want me,' she declared, 'you won't go. You won't even hide those men. If you promise not to do any of this and if you promise not to leave, on Sunday I will go with you to Lascande and we will do it again.'

'Don't use sex to bargain with me, Ari.'

'Die, then,' she retorted. 'See if I care. I'll never forgive you.'

She swung herself into the holm oak and when he called goodbye she did not turn around.

❧

In the shadow of the lane which marked the corner of the house, Romy began to breathe again.

On these balmy nights of early summer he liked to stand near her window, in the narrow lane where for years he had waited for her on the way to school. She would think him pathetic if she knew. *He* thought himself pathetic. But there were few enough thrills in Romy Dulac's life and nothing compared to this, being close to where on moonlit nights Arianne climbed out of her bedroom window into the arms of her waiting lover. They kissed just a few feet away from where he lurked in the gloom of the lane and he imagined it was *his* lips pressed against hers, his arms holding her. *I'll never forgive you.* Ha!

Luc almost brushed his shoulder as he hurried down the lane, but he did not seem to notice. *Some agent.* Romy smirked, though he could imagine only too well how he would feel in Luc's place. To have had Arianne and then to lose her . . . He waited a long time in the darkness to make sure Luc would not return, and as he waited his sense of triumph grew. Life would resume as it had before. They would walk together to school, she would press his arm with her small hand, she would listen to him again . . . He sped home as fast as his leg would let him. The dogs set to barking when he reached his parents' yard but he didn't even try to shush them.

## II

*Heading north,* wrote Alois on the platform at Montauban. The station about him teemed with activity. Railway porters staggering under the weight of metal trunks, hawkers, girls in high heels wearing too much lipstick, all mingled with the sea of grey uniforms, the kit and arsenal being loaded on to the train. Alois Grand had learned a long time ago to do no more than what was expected of him. He did not help but sat on his own kit bag with his writing pad on his knees. Cigarette smoke stung his eyes as he leaned forward to write.

'*A week of rest and decent cooking and we are a different unit, with fresh blood come to swell our ranks. We old-timers look more grizzled than the new recruits, but we are just as fit. The Captain says it will be good to do some real soldiering again, after Russia. We are going to fight* the Americans. We will lose – everyone knows we will lose – but we will be close to home and soon I will be with you again.'

The train was ready to leave. Alois's carriage was overcrowded and dark but he had claimed a seat by the window, and he carried on writing, using the tip of his cigarette to light the page while all around him his fellow soldiers drifted off to sleep.

'Things I'm looking forward to about coming home,' wrote Alois. 'Good coffee. Your schnitzels. Cinnamon rolls on Sunday mornings. Civilian clothes.'

The train ground to a halt. The men in the carriage stirred. Some of them got up to pee. Alois kept on writing.

'Remember when Wolf had scarlet fever?' he wrote. 'And you were nursing him, and one of the things you did was you picked a rose to put by his bed. I asked you what the point was and you said, it won't cure him but it might make him feel better. And when he woke up he smiled because the first thing he saw was that rose. More and more I think that it is these small gestures that matter most. The things we have done, my darling, that I hope you never know! And yet every morning our Captain shaves in a bowl of hot water. Every day another comrade reads his Bible, and every day I write to you. Small things, but they remind us who we are.

I never looked at the people I killed but when I sleep my

*dreams give them the faces of my beloved – you, Wolf, my*
*parents. I am coming back to you so tainted, so tainted . . .*
*My love for you both is the only good thing left about me,*
*and yet how can I touch you with these bloody hands? I have*
*made a pact with myself. No more killing between here and*
*home. I don't know how I'll do it, but I want – ah, impos-*
*sible! I want to be good.*

They were on the move again, and Alois was growing
drowsy.

*Soon,* he wrote. He folded the letter and slipped it
into the breast pocket of his uniform. *Soon, soon, soon,*
screeched the train, and he drifted off to sleep.

❧

The explosion ripped through the darkness as the train
rounded a bend between two hills, in a quiet stretch of
countryside some ten kilometres from Samaroux. Sheets
of flame reached for the stars, showers of sparks fell
down from them. Brakes screamed, metal shrieked. In
the copse where he waited, Luc shielded his ears and
eyes with his arms.

'How's the hunting tonight?'

Two men, hats pulled down over their faces, heavy
rucksacks on their backs. One grimacing with his hands
pressed against his side, the other alert, his hand clutching a knife.

'I haven't seen any wild boar,' responded Luc.

The man shielded his knife. 'Picot,' he said. 'This is Baptiste. He was still too close when we blew the line. He's bleeding badly. We'll have to support him. Let's go.'

They disappeared into the woods.

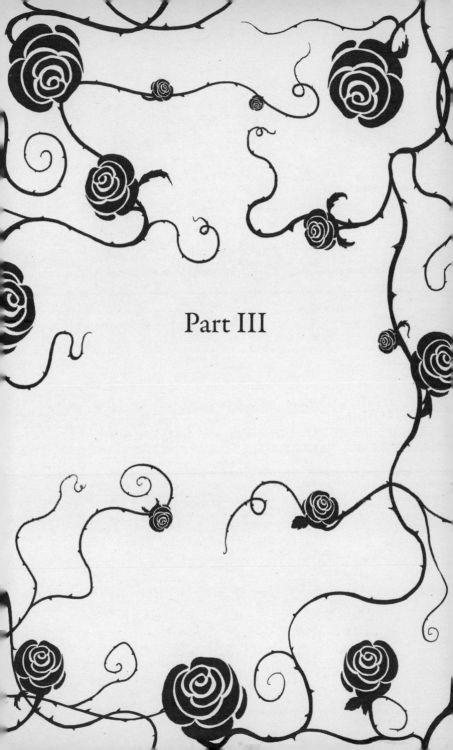

Part III

# June 10th, 1944

*I love it here now more than I ever did before. I love the landscape, the old stones of the houses, the rounded hills and the dark woods, the birdsong and the river. It used to drive me mad but now I love the fact that nothing ever happens.*

*Spring was beautiful this year, summer long and hot, but the season is on the turn now. The irises in the meadow have faded to brown, thin and dry as paper. Soon there will be nothing left of them but the stems waiting for next year, when it will all begin again. The crop fields are reverting to stubble, brown and bare. The earth is beginning to yield its harvest.*

*Except that now there is no need for food.*

*I am the only one left to tell you this story.*

*Listen to me. This is how it happened.*

# Morning

## I

Elodie had to call Arianne three times to get her out of bed.

'I'll wallop you!' she yelled up the stairs. 'Don't think you're too old for walloping!'

The door to the attic bedroom creaked open and Paul's tousled head appeared around the frame.

'She sent me to tell you there's no school today.'

'And don't think that means you can laze around all day!' shouted Elodie. Arianne rolled her eyes. Paul stepped into the room.

'You're dressed,' she said. 'Are *you* going to school?'

He pulled a face. 'Mine's not closed. It's not like it's a holiday or anything. Apparently there's been this train crash, so there are loads of soldiers in town and there's to be "no public meetings". And school's like a public meeting. Apparently.'

'That's rotten luck for you.' Arianne fought to keep her voice steady.

'Don't you want to know more about the crash?'

'Tell me.'

'You know where the track comes round the bend, just before the bridge where Papa sometimes took us for picnics? It got blown up last night. Ari, are you all right?'

'I'm fine.'

'Only you've gone really pale.'

'I said I'm fine.'

'Will you write me a note so I can skip school?'

'What, after last time?' Arianne managed a smile. 'Auntie'll only find out again. And personally I could do without a month of extra chores.'

'*You* cut school the other day.'

She flushed. 'That's beside the point. And you're not supposed to know about it.'

She stood up and walked across the bare floorboards to open the window. Behind her, she heard Paul kick the bedroom door, but she felt too weary to reason with him.

'Just go to school, there's a dear,' she said. 'And let me get dressed.'

'Will you see Luc today?'

'I don't know.'

'I heard you come in last night.'

'You really should learn to mind your own business.'

'Paul!' Elodie was climbing the stairs. Arianne tried to steady her breathing.

'*Paul!*'

'Look, I'm sorry,' said Arianne, but her brother had already gone.

≈

She picked up her clothes from the floor where she had dumped them last night, struggled into them and ran downstairs, tying a scrap of ribbon around her un-brushed hair as she went.

'So you're up.'

Arianne, noting that Paul was not in the kitchen, hes-itated before beating a retreat, aware that Elodie's sharp black eyes had noted every detail of her appearance.

'I need to find Paul.'

'I sent him up to wash.'

'I'll just go and . . .'

'Stay!' Elodie's feet, when she sat against the backrest of her chair, did not reach the ground. Arianne fixed her gaze upon her great-aunt's slippers, swinging beneath a pair of fragile ankles.

'Teresa Belleville came to find me after matins this morning in a terrible state. Luc's not been home all night.'

'*What?*'

'I don't suppose you know anything about that?'

'No,' mumbled Arianne.

'I won't have trouble,' said Elodie.

The slippers were an abomination against Elodie's sense of style, an indoor concession to her bunions. They were beginning to come apart at the seams. Arianne dragged her gaze away from her great-aunt's feet to look her in the eye.

'There's no trouble,' she said. Paul stomped into the room, saving her from further comment.

'I'm clean,' he announced.

Elodie gave a satisfied nod. Paul sat down to breakfast.

'Is there any fresh bread?'

'We're out of tokens.' Elodie was scurrying around the kitchen, sweeping an assortment of objects – glasses, keys, comb – into her handbag. 'Arianne, it's my day at the presbytery. I want you to clean the house from top to bottom, and I want you to go to the butcher's and queue for the *andouillette* he's been promising me for three weeks.'

'Is that all?' asked Arianne.

'And you can give Paul his lunch.'

Arianne smiled at her brother. 'I'll make you some eggy bread with the old crusts if you pick up some milk on your way home.'

'Milk!' Elodie snorted. 'As if milk could just be *picked up*! As if it flowed from taps!'

'You know Paul can get hold of anything,' said

131

Arianne. He finally met her eyes. The corners of his mouth twitched.

'I won't have thieving,' cried Elodie, but her great-niece and nephew had left the kitchen and were in the hall, hunting for his boots.

'Don't be cross,' said Arianne when he was ready. 'I can't bear it.'

He threw his arms around her waist. She hugged him back. He smelled of sweat and grass.

'I'll see you at lunch,' she said. 'Be good.'

∂◦

Paul's sense of injury got the better of him within minutes of leaving home. He loved Arianne more than anything in the world. More than wandering through the woods on a day like this, more than his new knife, more even than Thierry Legros's hunting bitch's recent litter of pups, but a few months ago, when he was still the whole world to her, she would never have spoken to him like she had this morning. Besides, the day really did promise to be a corker, and *she* didn't have to go to school. Making sure no one could see him, he slipped off the road to school into a side-street next to the church, emptied the contents of his bag into a hollow wall he liked to use, and melted into the forest.

The rabbit at his first snare was still alive. He didn't

enjoy finishing them off, but it was a necessary evil. He grabbed this one with both hands, pulled the neck and gave it a sharp twist. It broke with a satisfying crunch. By the time the bell rang for morning lessons, school was a distant memory.

## II

Romy never set an alarm. Why should he, with his mother always there to wake him? His first thought when she came in was for Arianne. His second was that the light streaming in through his windows – he always slept with his shutters open – was brighter than it should be.

'It's half-past seven.' His mother's voice was not much more than a whisper, the result of twenty-five years of marriage to his father. 'There's no school today. I would have let you sleep, but your father wants to talk to you when he's finished opening the mill.'

'Oh God.' Romy's heart sank. 'What does he want now?'

She set about tidying his room, a pointless task because he would only *un*tidy it when she was gone. He liked his things to be just so, but had learned from long experience that it was pointless telling her. She moved from the collection of birds' eggs on his mantelpiece to his desk.

'Don't look at those! he cried. She was holding his latest poems, his hopeless attempts at a sonnet to Arianne. 'Give them to me!'

*She must be bad today*, he thought, as his mother tucked his handwritten pages into a physics textbook, stacking *that* with a pile of detective novels.

'There was an accident last night.' She looked at him at last with troubled eyes. The last light had left them when his brothers left. The shadow of her latest bruise was still visible beneath her cheekbone. 'They're saying there was a bomb on the railway track, a train came off the rails. An awful lot of people died. I think he wants to talk to you about that.'

She would have stayed to help him dress if he had let her. He had to push her out of the room and even then he could hear her hovering outside his door. He limped over to his wardrobe. He would visit Arianne later, once the boring business with his father was over, and he wanted to look his best.

He finished dressing and opened his window. The saws down at the mill were running. His father would be home soon. People would be pressing him for answers, and he would be squeezing his informants, including his son, for information. Jo Dulac never cared too much about the truth of the reports he gave. The Milice needed guilty verdicts as surely as murderers needed victims. It didn't really matter who paid the price, as long as somebody did. The ghost of an idea began to form in Romy's mind, but he threw it out at once.

Joan of Arc would never betray one of her own.


### III

'So what happens now?'

One of the new privates, just out of school by the look of him, sat by Alois Grand's side, huddled in a blanket. The bandage wrapped around his head in the early hours by an overwrought medic was already slipping down over his eye, making him look even younger. He pushed it back up with an impatient gesture and bit his lip as he surveyed the makeshift camp the Captain's men had set up a hundred yards from the railway line in the aftermath of the explosion.

'Why are we still here?' he asked.

'We're waiting.' Alois was skinning a rabbit and did not look up as he replied.

'But why *us*? There were thousands of men on that train. They all left in trucks this morning. Those who weren't dead.'

'I think you'll find the dead went in those trucks as well. Or didn't you see them?'

The young man shuddered at the memory – the worst of the wounded loaded into ambulances on stretchers, the dead thrown into closed trucks wrapped in makeshift shrouds. He stuck out his chin, stubbornly.

'Why are *we* still here?' he repeated.

'Mind yourself.' Alois held the rabbit up by its ears and slit it from breast to arse. Blood and innards spilled out, splashing the young man's boots. 'Captain caught these this morning,' he said. 'There's not a lot stops the Captain from going hunting. Not even something like last night. Even in Russia, he hunted most mornings.'

The private's name was Jonas Bucher. His literature professor at school had had a secret fondness for the Russian nineteenth-century novel, and shared his enthusiasm with a few selected students. He found that he could quite easily imagine the Captain galloping on horseback across a frozen steppe. Jonas had no love of army life, but he couldn't deny that men like the Captain gave it a certain *frisson*.

'I would love to see Russia,' he sighed.

Alois Grand's eyes, as black as the Captain's were blue, fixed him with their famous stare. 'Aye, well.' He shrugged, and turned his attention back to the rabbits. 'Reckon Russia'd be nice enough without a bloody great war in the middle of it.'

He roasted the meat on skewers pulled from his kitbag, and they ate it sandwiched between pieces of French bread, washed down with thin coffee. The Captain returned at the wheel of an Army jeep just as they were finishing, a nervous-looking man in French Milice uniform at his side and two armed privates in the back.

'Got us a little investigation in the area,' he called out to Alois. 'Orders from on high.'

Alois Grand grunted. Jonas Bucher looked at him in surprise. The big man's fists were clenched, his knuckles white.

'I need a fluent French speaker. Preferably one who can drive as well.'

'I speak French!' Jonas Bucher scrambled to his feet and saluted. His bandage slipped down again over his eye.

'Climb aboard then, soldier!' The Captain laughed and leaned out to pluck the bandage from Jonas's head. 'Can't have an invalid driving me.'

Alois closed his hand over the open window of the jeep. He had a fleeting vision of himself immobilising it, locked in an eternal battle of wills with the Captain.

He cleared his throat. His mouth was dry. 'When do we head north?' he asked.

'All in good time,' said the Captain. 'How was the rabbit?'

Alois let go of the car.

'We saved you some,' he muttered.

'I'm not hungry. You know it's the sport I like,' said the Captain. He tossed his head at the French *milicien*, indicating he should get into the back. 'When you're ready, soldier.'

The Captain waved as the jeep leaped forward. Alois wiped his skewers on a cloth and announced that he was going to wash.

⁂

A stream ran amongst the trees. He followed its course upriver until the incline steepened and he came to a place where a pool had formed. He fell to one knee, plunged his hands into the water and splashed his face several times before standing again to undress.

He had jarred his shoulder in the crash and winced as he unbuttoned his shirt. Somewhere behind him a twig snapped and he whirled round to face the noise, pulling his revolver from its holster. Another snap, and he caught sight of the rear end of a doe. The gun returned to its holster. Alois dropped to his knees.

Clara loved the river back home, even when it was raining and the mist hid it from view. She could walk for hours, pressed up against him under an umbrella, guessing at the silhouettes of the container ships sailing inland from the North Sea.

'Did you see it? Wasn't it amazing?'

'Amazing.'

The memory felt more like a dream. He hadn't seen

the point then of ships one could not see but now, closer to home than he had been for years, he was beginning to understand. Something to do, he thought, with faith and with believing.

Birdsong, the gurgling of the stream, a breeze rustling the forest canopy. Alois Grand hugged his knees to his chest and closed his eyes, opened them and thought he caught a glimpse of something, a woman's dress, a sheet of white blonde hair. He thought he heard her call and turned his head in the direction of the sound. Somewhere in the forest, a bird's cry made a mockery of his imaginings.

It was not Clara. How could it have been? Alois lay full length on the bank of moss and plunged his head into the icy stream. Water tumbled on to the back of his neck. He closed his eyes and didn't come up until he saw stars.

## IV

Any minute his father would be home. Romy checked his reflection in the mirror. He liked the way the new hairdresser in town had cut his hair so that it swept in a wing across his forehead. His horn-rimmed glasses made him look intellectual rather than plain short-sighted, and his best shirt, with only one small mend under the collar, was crisp and freshly laundered. Compared to most of the youth of Samaroux, he was positively foppish.

A door slammed downstairs, followed by the sound of footsteps. Romy leaped away from the mirror. His bedroom door flew open.

'Where were you last night?' His father never did waste time with preliminaries.

'I don't know what you mean.'

'After curfew.'

'Nowhere.'

'Don't give me *nowhere*. I heard you come in, the racket you made. Where were you?'

'Walking.'

'Where?'

'In the woods.'

'Why?'

'It was nice. It was . . . poetic.'

'Bleeding poetic!' His father's fist shot out and cuffed him round the ear. 'You look like a pansy with your hair like that.'

'Thanks.'

'Where were you?'

'I told you, in the woods. This conversation . . .'

'Where? When? Why?'

'. . . is going round in circles.'

'I'll give you circles.'

Romy smirked. A mistake. His father stepped closer.

Nostrils flared, he looked like a bull about to charge. Romy took a step back.

'I want to be proud of you, son.'

'Yes, sir.'

'And you do know what happened last night? Your mother told you?'

'Yes, sir!'

'And you heard nothing, on your *poetic* walk? Nothing that made you think, *that's a bit odd*? Nothing you think the people investigating this incident – they *will* investigate, you know they will – might consider interesting?'

His second's falter was enough. Jo grabbed him by the wrist.

'You know something.'

'You're hurting me!'

'I'll hurt you a whole lot more if you don't tell me what it is.'

'It's nothing . . . Ow!'

Romy staggered towards the bed, nursing his wrist. Jo leaned against the doorframe, waiting.

'You know what'll happen if you don't say.'

No, thought Romy, I don't know. I don't know if you will beat me or take it out on Mother, use the horse-whip or your fists. I don't know if you will lock me in the cellar or in my room. He remembered Arianne's voice last night – proud, full of unshed tears – and stood a little taller. He might hate Luc and fear his father, but he would never betray her.

His father pushed himself away from the door and began to walk across the room. Romy shrank.

It wasn't even as if he knew that much. Could he say just a little, enough to appease his father?

'Well?' asked his father.

'I heard a quarrel,' whispered Romy.

'What about?'

'I don't know.'

'Who was it?'

'It was just a man, I mean a boy. And a girl.' He fell silent. His father sighed.

'Tell me this isn't about Arianne Lafayette? Don't waste my time.'

Romy fixed a point on the floor just short of his father's boots.

'Girl like her, she's never even going to know you exist. And do you know why?'

Perhaps, if he blinked, the tear collecting in the corner of his eye would not run down the length of his nose as it was threatening to do.

'Because you're a loser. A pathetic, useless human being. What were you doing? Listening at her window, hoping to hear her at it with her lover?'

The tear exploded into a circle on the floor. Others followed. He did not dare look up.

'What was the quarrel about?'

Still Romy stared at the floor. He steeled himself for blows, but none came. He heard the door open. 'Don't leave your room.'

Romy drew his knees into his chest and wept.

## V

Today was supposed to be as normal as possible, wasn't that what Luc had said? So why hadn't he come home last night? He would be all right – wouldn't he? She had no proof that the train crash was his doing. She tried to recall his exact words. *Two men. I have to meet them and hide them.* Not, *I have to blow up a train.* Would he have told her, if that had been the case? And did he even know how to blow up a train? What if . . .

Arianne howled and shook her head to dispel images of Luc captured, Luc wounded, Luc lying dead somewhere in the forest. Luc was probably at Lascande, so carried away by his own heroism he didn't see the point in coming home. Unless it was her fault, for not being nicer to him . . . She threw off the apron she had donned to placate Elodie before she left, grabbed a basket and braced herself to go out. Doubts assailed her as she opened the front door. What if Luc were to come while she was out? Would he wait? She should leave him a note. But saying what? And surely a note smacked of desperation? She compromised by leaving a notepad and pencil in the middle of the kitchen table, and the back door unlocked. If he came, *he* could leave *her* a note! And she wouldn't be long if she managed to avoid the queues.

Perhaps, she thought hopefully as she walked towards the shops, it was all a mistake. Perhaps, trying to clear his mind after the night's activities, he had gone for a run in the woods this morning. He often did that when there wasn't school. It was perfectly possible that he had slipped out without waking his mother, and not returned before she left for morning church. Probably right now he was home, eating breakfast, planning to come and find her. Possibly he was going to apologise and tell her he had changed his mind about leaving tonight.

She tried not to look for him too obviously, but strained to catch a glimpse of him from the corner of her eye. No sign, and though she had not expected one, she was disappointed. She picked up the dried split peas Elodie wanted at the general stores, toyed with the idea of running home then shrugged and joined the butcher's queue.

A hand tapped her on the shoulder. She whirled around, but her face fell at the sight of her cousin.

'No class.' Solange beamed. 'So good.'

'So good,' Arianne assented.

'The parents are being awfully gloomy about the whole business, but I was thinking about a picnic. What do you think? Will you come with Luc? I'll try and gather a bunch of jolly people.'

'I don't know.'

'Ah, go on! You two never do things with the rest of us!'

'This queue's taking forever.'

'Ari, are you all right?'

Arianne's face crumpled.

'Something's wrong,' said Solange.

'We just had a fight.'

'But you two are OK? I mean, if *you* two aren't OK . . .'

Gaspard Félix appeared at the door of his shop to announce he had run out of meat. The queue dispersed, muttering.

'He promised Auntie an *andouillette*. She's been waiting ages.'

'Sneak round the back of the shop when everyone's gone. We don't have to do the picnic, you know. We can just spend the afternoon together if you'd rather, just the two of us. It's ages since we did that.'

'No, have your picnic.'

Solange looked hurt. Arianne kissed her and she brightened. 'Shall I call round anyway, in case you want to come?'

'Do that . . .' Arianne trailed off. Teresa Belleville had

just stepped out of the baker's shop further up the street. 'I have to go.'

She called out as she drew closer, but either Luc's mother did not hear or she did not want to talk. By the time Arianne reached her house, the door was already shut.

There was no point asking her anyway. It didn't matter if Luc was home or not. She would stick to her guns. If he wanted her, he could come and get her himself.

⁓

Father Julien sat with Jarvis outside the Café du Commerce, wishing the mayor would stop asking difficult questions.

'It had nothing to do with anyone in the village, nothing at all,' he repeated.

'Who, then?'

'What are you so worried about?'

'What am I *worried* about?' The mayor stared at the old priest incredulously. 'Didn't you hear about what happened at Tulle? The reprisals there?'

'That was a completely different situation. There was a battle, hand-to-hand combat.'

'*They hanged over a hundred people*. From *lamp posts*. As your mayor, I am ordering you to tell me what this village's involvement was with last night's explosion.'

'I've already told you. Nothing.'

'I know you're hiding something.'

Father Julien sighed. 'Léon, as your oldest friend, believe me when I say you know all you need to know. The men who blew up the tracks came from a different region altogether. By tonight, they will have left the area. They are nowhere in the village. The explosion took place ten kilometres from here, there is nothing to link it to us. As mayor of this village, it behoves you to keep calm. It would do no good at all if people saw you panic, no good at all.'

'So what was your involvement? Why would you even know about any of this, if it had nothing to do with you?'

The old priest shifted in his chair.

'Julien?' said the mayor. 'I know you're hiding something, and I know you're worried.'

'I was asked to send someone to see them safe.'

'Oh for pity's sake!'

'This is important work, Léon!' Father Julien leaned forward in his chair and clutched Jarvis's sleeve. 'Anything which slows the progress of German troops towards the north . . . This is our time, don't you see? Now is when we must draw on our reserves of courage, strike down the enemy in our land, stand shoulder to shoulder with our allies . . .'

'Who did you send?' asked Jarvis.

'You know I can't . . .'

'Who?' hissed Jarvis.

'Luc Belleville,' muttered the priest.

'That child! That impetuous, hot-headed . . .'

'He is not as hot-headed as you think,' said Father Julien. 'I have been preparing him for months, and I believe he is ready.'

'Where is he now?'

Father Julien said nothing.

'*Julien?*'

'He never came home this morning,' admitted the old priest.

'Jesus,' said Jarvis. 'Dear God and Christ Almighty.'

Together they watched Teresa Belleville cross the market square.

'Go and talk to her,' said Jarvis.

Father Julien grimaced as he drained his cup. He never would get used to the taste of chicory.

'I'm sure there's a perfectly good explanation,' he said.

'There had better be, my friend.' Jarvis's usually genial face was sombre. 'For all our sakes, there had better be.'

## VI

Romy obeyed his father, of course he did. When had he ever done anything but? He was still in his room and

148

still moping when the Captain arrived, accompanied by the Milice officer and Jonas Bucher.

He opened his window to listen as his mother went out to greet them. The Milicien, Officer Plondier, knew his parents well. He did the talking. The soldiers – a private and a captain, Romy recognised the uniforms – stood beside him. The private held a notepad and pen. The captain frowned as he followed the conversation.

'We are looking for two men,' said Plondier.

'We've not seen anyone here.'

'We need to talk to your husband.'

The delivery boy was sent to the mill to fetch his father, who arrived minutes later. The Milicien introduced the officers and explained their visit. Last night's explosion, two men seen running from the scene, no clues. They were investigating all the neighbouring villages. Could he help?

The occupying army being hungry for wood, Jo Dulac had done well out of the war. Orders had doubled over the years of the Occupation and even if prices were lower and credit terms more awkward than he might like, he wasn't complaining. His boys were earning real wages in a proper German factory and there was bread and meat on his table. He knew what people said about him in the village, but he didn't care. War was war. What mattered was being on the right side, and if that meant landing others in it – well, they were asking for it anyway. He took a personal pride in always having an answer, but this morning's interrogations of his usual spies had drawn a blank.

'Gentlemen, I'm afraid I can't help,' he said, and Romy savoured his discomfiture – the way he held out his hands, so obviously the underdog! 'I've heard of nothing last night but a teenage lovers' tiff.'

'Ah, young love.' The Captain's voice was gentle, his French accented but correct. 'So painful.'

Nobody seemed to know quite how to react to this. Romy smirked. The others looked away but the Captain was already walking back towards the jeep, settling himself in the passenger seat with every appearance of *ennui*.

'We'll be off then,' said the younger man, also in French. 'Sorry to have troubled you. Officer Plondier says you have been very helpful in the past.'

Plondier shook Jo Dulac by the hand. 'Could have been anyone,' he muttered when the others were out of earshot. 'We got no warning about this one. Don't be fooled by that Captain, neither. We've been around every village in a fifteen-kilometre radius and he's hopping mad. Frankly, it don't matter who did it. Any old scapegoat will do.'

'Look into it, Monsieur Dulac,' called the Captain as the jeep moved off. 'This lover's tiff. You never know. A jilted lover is always – ah, my French is so rusty – like a loose cannon, I think that is the expression. I don't care for cannons. Bring me news, shall we say, ah, before noon?'

The jeep took off in a cloud of exhaust. Jo turned back towards the house. Up in his room, Romy grabbed his boots.

'Romy!'

If he was quick, he could clear the landing passage and be out of the back door before his father reached the top of the front staircase.

'*Romy!*'

Jo erupted on the landing and roared at the sight of the empty room. Romy was gone, flying down the back stairs as fast as his gammy leg allowed him. His mother's bicycle was leaning against the wall. He seized it and leaped into the saddle.

By the time his father burst out of the house, Romy was gone.

VII

The Captain's men had moved on after breakfast, piled into a convoy of trucks which carted them and their salvageable material a few kilometres across country to the edge of a lake where they had come to another halt. Tailgates were lowered and men jumped down, scattering around the shore to smoke or stretch their legs. There was room in the truck now to lie back. Alois turned up his collar and closed his eyes, tilting his head to the sky. Sunlight warmed his face.

Shadows over water, dawn breaking over the countryside, stars in the night sky above their cottage. The high notes of the flute she played so well.

Clara. Her name meant light.

The first time he saw her, she was standing with the sun behind her on the threshold of his forge, her dress a flimsy halo around her body, all long limbs and smooth curves, her features lost to the shadows. He blinked as she stepped into the forge and became more though not wholly ordinary, a fragile body in a simple dress, dark gold hair smoothed in the nape of her neck, the scent of bergamot and roses. 'I've come about Frau Blume's firescreen.'

Her eyes were violet coloured, he saw.

'You *are* Alois Grand, the blacksmith?'

The screen was imitation Art Deco, black mesh with pewter flowers, copied from a picture of a country house her mother had shown him in a magazine. He had never made anything like it before.

'You're an artist.'

'I wouldn't say that.'

She ran her fingers over the mesh of the screen before tracing the contours of a wrought-iron tulip.

'I wish I could make something like this.'

'I could teach you if you like.'

Nine years later, he still couldn't believe he had said that. The thought of her in the forge! That hair streaked with sweat, those curves beneath a leather apron, that face reddened by work!

'I would love that.'

She smiled. He smiled back.

❧

'What are you looking so happy about?'

The Captain had returned. Alois ignored his question.

'What do we do now?' he asked.

'We wait.'

'What for?' asked Jonas Bucher.

The older men turned to stare at him.

'For orders,' said the Captain. 'What else?'

## VIII

Arianne was in the garden collecting vegetables to cook with the knuckle of ham she had managed to extract from the butcher in lieu of the *andouillette*, when Father Julien appeared at the gate.

'I am looking,' he announced, 'for Luc.'

'Well, he's not here.'

'I'm a little worried he doesn't seem to be *anywhere*.'

'*You're* worried? Don't make me laugh.'

'I'm not sure I know what you mean.'

'There's no point pretending.' Arianne glared at him. 'I know all about your little circus.'

'Oh dear.' Father Julien walked over to sit on the garden bench, removed his glasses and rubbed his eyes. Arianne followed him, merciless.

'Last night,' she said. 'The bomb.'

'It's best if we don't talk about it.'

'That's rich.'

'What did he tell you?'

'Is he hurt?'

'I don't know.'

'Oh God!' Arianne's hands flew to her face. 'He's dead, I know he's dead!'

'This is disastrous,' said Father Julien.

Arianne jumped to her feet. 'I have to go and look for him. I have to find him.'

Father Julien gripped her by the wrist. 'You have to stay here.'

'How *can* I?' she cried.

'*Think*, Arianne! A hot-headed young man, well-known for his shame of his collaborationist grandfather, who makes a public scene at the arrest of a Jewish family and disappears days later, the morning after an explosion on the railway causes the death of numerous German soldiers? The Milice are already crawling all over the countryside. It won't take them long to put two and two together.'

'Just let me run to Lascande to see if he's there,' she pleaded.

'No, Arianne! Do you think they won't know about you? Do you think, when they find you roaming alone in the woods, they won't know you are out looking for him, and use you to lead them to the men he is hiding?'

'But they could find me here!'

'Better that. I can protect you here. Now, I've spoken to his mother. Luc left last night on the last train to visit family in the south. She would have gone herself but she hasn't been well. There was no time for him to say good-bye, we don't know when he'll be back. Is that clear?'

'Luc hates his family in the south.'

Father Julien tightened his grip on her wrist. 'I said, is that clear?'

There was no sign now of the jovial priest who had taken her to the Bellevilles' party only a few weeks before. His ferocity might have seemed comical had she not been so afraid.

'If Luc is hurt or killed, there is nothing you can do. They'll be watching you. Believe me, they're not stupid. Swear by Almighty God you will not go. If they have any reason to suspect anyone in this village, any reason at all, the consequences will be dire. Swear it!'

Arianne sobbed. 'I swear.'

'Good.' He hesitated as he prepared to go through the gate. 'Faith and love, child. This is when we need to be strong.' He drew the sign of the cross over her head and was gone.

## IX

Jo Dulac didn't go straight after his son. Instead he made a detour through the village and stopped to speak to Teresa Belleville.

'He's not here,' she said when she came to the door.

'Where is he, then?'

'He's gone south to visit family,' she said calmly. 'Not that it's any of your business.'

*Like hell,* thought Jo. He ran into a group of lads off for a game of football and asked if they had seen Luc, but none of them had. Solange Lafayette was sunning herself on the market square with some other girls. She told him nothing either, but her cool gaze faltered when he asked if she knew about the boy's quarrel with her cousin.

He pressed on to Arianne's house but fell back when he saw her in the garden talking to Father Julien – he never had liked the priest, his way of looking at you as if your soul were on display. Jo had nothing to reproach himself with but still, a man's soul was his own. The girl trudged back into the house when the priest was gone, and just by the way she walked he knew the boy wasn't with her. Time was pressing on. He weighed up his chances – Arianne Lafayette or his son, who was more likely to squeal?

There was no contest.

⁂

The fountain in the woods had been a gift to the parish from its priest in 1837. It boasted naked cherubs with broken harps, a faded statue of the Virgin Mary and a square pool at ground level, thick with weeds. Romy had never understood why a priest would donate a fountain, nor why having donated it he would choose it to be built such an impractical distance from the village.

The bench beside the fountain was damp and the air was cold. His throat began to hurt, the legacy of an untreated bout of tonsillitis the previous winter. It wasn't much of a hiding place, but he had run here often as a child to escape a beating and he couldn't think of anywhere else to go. He closed his eyes and wondered – not for the first time – what would happen to him when he got home. He couldn't think now what running away had achieved.

'Useless.'

So his father had found him.

'Did you really think I wouldn't remember this place?'

'I didn't think you cared,' muttered Romy, but Jo had him by the ear and was dragging him towards the road.

'Where are we going?' he asked.

'Your lover boy's vanished,' said Jo.

'So?'

'Stop messing about.' Jo had brought his beloved pre-war Renault out for the occasion. He shoved Romy into the passenger seat and started the engine. 'You wouldn't have run if you didn't know something.'

The car broke down a few hundred yards short of where the Germans had set up their new camp beside the lake and they had to continue their journey on foot. Romy asked no more questions. He knew that in his father's mind there was a dignity to a motorised entrance, even if the engine *was* powered by a wood-burning generator. What with Romy's limp and the sweat rings flowering beneath his father's armpits, turning up on foot just didn't have the same authority.

They had reached the Limoges road. From their vantage point higher up the hill, he could see an agglomeration of khaki vehicles and men in *feldgrau* uniforms. He was reminded, absurdly, of the summer camps he had so loathed as a child.

'I suppose you think this is wrong.' Jo Dulac came

to stand beside his son. 'Telling on a school friend. You want to do the brave and decent thing.'

'Luc Belleville is not my friend,' said Romy, 'but I don't understand what it is you think he's done.'

'He's gone missing, that's what he's done. Look at you, standing up for your girl's lover, all selfless and noble. Even if he hasn't done anything yet, he will one day. So we shop him. They go after him and leave the rest of us alone.'

'I've got nothing to say to you. And even if I did, I'm not a grass.'

'A grass?'

Jo grabbed his son's jaw and leaned into him, so close Romy could smell the sourness of his breath. 'Is that what you think I am? Little coward. I fought in the last war. I've seen what people do to each other, given half the chance. Heard of Tulle, hero? They hanged a hundred civilians there last week, and sent another five hundred to the camps. I don't grass, son, I contain. I give them what they want and stop the rot from spreading. You'll do the same if you know what's good for you.'

'I don't know where he is!'

*On Sunday I will go with you to Lascande.* Something about the way she had said it. On *Sunday*. As opposed to now. *Oh God*.

'You do know,' said Jo. 'I've never seen you look so guilty. And you'll tell that Captain what he needs to know, even if I have to beat it out of you. If you make a fool of me now, I'll kill you with my own hands.'

They found the officer who had come that morning sitting on a fallen tree trunk by the edge of the forest, cleaning a rifle. A big man sat beside him, apparently writing a letter. Jo coughed. The Captain looked up and frowned.

'Do I know you?' he asked in French.

*He's forgotten!* Romy's heart soared. *He's actually forgotten us!*

Jo cleared his throat again. He looked smaller here. He might have done better than others out of the war, but compared to the Captain and this colossus he looked as ragged as the rest of them. Even now he was tugging at the sleeve of his jacket, twisting it round to conceal the more obvious mend, the one which ran along the inside seam from his wrist all the way up to his elbow.

'You came to us earlier,' he said, and this time Romy winced at his obvious fawning. 'I own the sawmill up at Samaroux. You asked me to investigate a quarrel. A lovers' tiff?' Spoken out loud, the words sounded ridiculous, but the Captain's brow cleared in recognition.

'*Informant,*' he told the big man. Romy winced again. 'Well?'

'My son.' Jo cleared his throat again. 'My son overheard something.'

They were all looking at him.

'I . . .'

The Captain sighed. Jo Dulac glared at his son.

'It was nothing, really . . .'

The Captain's fingers were long and tapered, his nails shaped and polished. They would look at home wrapped around a champagne flute or a cigar, those fingers, playing the piano or the violin. Right now they were tapping the holster of his revolver. Romy gulped.

'Just tell me what you know,' suggested the Captain. The fingers had stopped drumming to settle on the handgrip of the revolver.

'Twenty-three German soldiers died last night.' Romy shivered. Did the man ever raise his voice? 'If you know something, you had better tell me. I can't answer for the consequences if you don't.'

'He's leaving,' Romy muttered. Even as he said this he knew that it would not be enough. The Captain raised an eyebrow.

'He wouldn't say where.' Romy stared at the ground as he spoke. 'She begged him and begged him to tell her, but he wouldn't say. I think he's going to join the Maquis.'

The Captain laughed. 'That's hardly news. Every able-bodied man in the country is trying to do the same. They all want to be heroes now the Americans are near, with their barefoot soldiers and the farm tools they use instead of guns.' He beckoned Romy closer and whispered against his ear. 'You're hiding something.'

Containment, his father had called it. He knew what Arianne would think of that. The bile rose from his stomach.

'Two men.' Romy's mouth was so dry he could barely speak. 'He had to hide them.'

'Where?'

'I don't know!' he wept. 'She asked and asked, but he wouldn't say where. She doesn't know, she kept asking, but he wouldn't say!'

'Who else knows?'

'Nobody,' stammered Romy. The Captain grabbed him by the collar and pressed his thumb into his throat. Jo stepped forward. The big man held him back.

'Who else?'

'He has a mother,' said Jo.

Romy staggered as the Captain released him and stood bent over, coughing.

'A mother,' said the Captain. 'Perhaps that will do.'

X

Arianne climbed the steep stairs up to her bedroom when Father Julien left and came to stand before her window.

Luc, stripped to the waist, standing in the stream with

the water gleaming on his sunburned skin. Lying in the long grass at Lascande and on the moonlit hill, his lips on her neck, her throat . . . He couldn't possibly be dead!

She left her window and walked across the room to her washstand. The mirror which hung above it was tarnished at the edges, but it was serviceable enough.

Was this what he saw when he looked at her? She reached round to undo the fastenings of her dress, letting it fall in a pool at her feet. Round shoulders, small breasts, the pleasing curve of her waist . . . Turning to look at herself from the side, she could see every one of her ribs in the mirror. Did he think her scrawny? She remembered the feel of his hands working their way down her back, vertebra by vertebra, the sweep of his fingers.

She threw herself on the bed. Her mother had hand-stitched her counterpane, an American-style quilt, as a present for her eighth birthday. Pink, white and green, made of different fabrics, with a square of rose-coloured toile at the centre on to which she had embroidered Arianne's initials in looping silk. Arianne had been ecstatic. *Thank goodness!* Marielle had laughed. *Because that is the last time I ever make anything like it!* She curled into a ball and pulled the counterpane close about her.

'Ari? Ari, where are you?' A clatter of feet on the stairs heralded Solange's eruption into the room, less groomed than usual in a summer dress and faded espadrilles, her blonde mane hanging down her back, her cheeks flushed from the run up the stairs.

'There you are! I couldn't find anyone for the picnic. Oh my God you're in your *underwear*! Is Luc here? Oh no, Ari, you've been *crying*!'

Solange threw herself to her knees by her cousin's bed and gathered her in her arms.

'There there,' she murmured. 'I'm here, I've got you. There, there.'

'You sound like your mother.' Arianne sniffed and attempted a smile.

'Sometimes, *chérie*, I *feel* like my mother. Now then. Talk to your Auntie Sol.'

Solange climbed on to the bed, lay down beside Arianne and pulled the counterpane over them both so that it covered their heads. 'Do you remember, we used to lie like this when we were little? Now, is this all about Luc?'

Arianne sniffed again.

'Did you know Jo Dulac was out looking for him? Where on earth is he?'

'He's gone south to visit his family,' whispered Arianne.

'What? He hates his family! Oh Ari, don't cry! Where is he really?'

'I don't know!' wailed Arianne. 'And I'm not allowed to look for him!'

'Who says you're not allowed?'

'I can't tell you.'

'And why not?'

'It's dangerous.'

'Yes, well. Luc *is* dangerous. That temper. We've known that since the beginning.'

The wind picked up outside and blew in through the open window. Arianne shivered despite the thick padding of the counterpane. Solange tightened her arms around her and thought of summer afternoons at Lascande, the blue horizon, the way the low rays of the sun played around Luc and Arianne's shadows, making them shimmer, giving them haloes.

'Where would you look for him, if you went? Where would you start?'

Arianne turned on to her side to look at her and smiled sadly.

Of course, thought Solange. Where else?

'You should go,' she declared. 'Right now, before you change your mind.'

'But Father Julien . . .'

'Shh . . .' Solange put a finger to her cousin's lips. 'Don't tell me. Ari, this is *Luc*. The boy who *lit you up inside,* who made you smile again? It doesn't matter what anybody says.'

She threw back the counterpane and jumped to her feet.

'Come on, Ari, right now!'

She held out her hand to help her cousin up.

'Now, do you have everything you need?' she asked seriously.

'Need?'

'You know!' Solange sighed. 'To stop the little babies...'

'Oh!' Arianne blushed. 'I didn't think of that.'

'Lucky you have me then! Maman's got everything you need at home. Not that she knows I know . . . Now, pull yourself together, wash your face, get dressed, brush your hair and I'll be back. It doesn't do to be unprepared.'

'You're mad!' Arianne started to laugh. Solange stopped by the bedroom door and beamed at her.

'I love you,' she said. 'I want you to be happy.'

Solange ran down the stairs, as noisily as she had come up. Arianne fell back against her pillow, still laughing.

## XI

'You will ride in with us,' said the Captain when Romy asked to return to the village.

'I would rather walk.'

'You will ride with us,' repeated the Captain as he strode away. Jo sat a little distance away on the ground. Romy was left alone with Alois Grand. The big man held out a packet of cigarettes. Romy hesitated before taking one and they smoked together in silence.

'This boy,' asked Alois at last. His French was slow and hesitant. 'He is your friend?'

'No!'

'The girl then.'

'She has done nothing wrong.'

'That wasn't my question.'

'Yes,' said Romy. 'She is my friend. At least, she was.'

He gazed around the camp, looking for a way out.

'There is nowhere to go.' Alois looked almost sorry. 'If you run, I will shoot you. I am afraid you are screwed, my friend. You are completely screwed.'

*Screwed*, Romy repeated to himself. *I'm sorry, I'm sorry, I'm sorry, I'm sorry.*

A new contingent of soldiers had arrived from the barracks at Limoges, fresher and better dressed than the tired men from the train. They came in a convoy of armoured vehicles, guns at the ready, with ammunition belts around their waists and shoulders. They stopped by the lake. A man in officer's uniform jumped out of the leading vehicle and strode towards the Captain.

'What are they talking about?' Romy asked Alois.

'Orders.'

'What orders?'

The big man shrugged again, 'To find our man. Wait and they will tell us.'

A cloud passed before the sun, blocking the light. A movement in the trees caught Romy's eye. He blinked. A small creature was crawling down the hill, and came to a stop behind a hawthorn bush. Romy glanced around to check nobody was watching and peered closer. The cloud moved on and a ray of sunlight fell upon the shaking bush, illuminating, for a split second, a head of unmistakable red. Romy's heart lurched.

'I need to pee.'

'So pee,' said Alois.

'Somewhere private?' He indicated his poor leg. 'It's not as if I could run away.'

The big man tossed his head towards the trees.

Romy limped with as much nonchalance as he could muster towards the woods, where he made a show of unbuttoning his flies, standing with his legs apart and his back to the camp.

'I need you to do something for me,' he muttered.

'Sod that,' said Paul. 'I don't run errands for turncoats.'

'This isn't a game!'

'Are you going to pee, or what? You look a right idiot with your willy hanging out like that.'

'It's the only way I could get away,' hissed Romy. 'I need you to get a message to your sister.'

'Suppose I just want to stay here and watch the soldiers?'

'I need you,' enunciated Romy, 'to run back to the village as fast as you possibly can, find your sister and tell her to run. Run and hide. Got it?'

Paul was listening now. 'What's she done?' he whispered.

'It's not her, it's her loser boyfriend. Run and hide. That's all. I've got to go or they'll smell a rat. Run, Paul. And don't screw up.'

He turned, praying that nobody was watching him or if they were, that they had not seen Paul. He needn't have worried. Every eye was turned towards the Captain, talking to them beside the lake from a makeshift platform in the back of a jeep. A light scamper from the bushes behind indicated that Paul was on his way. He felt himself go limp with relief.

Ten minutes later, the Germans were gone, flattened grass and the charred circles of their fires the only traces of their passage.

# Midday

## I

'Go now,' Solange had said. 'Before you change your mind.'

Arianne dressed quickly when her cousin had gone, though her fingers fumbled with her buttons and her shoes slipped several times from her hands. Quickly, quickly! She prayed that Luc was waiting for her at Lascande, that he had guessed she would come looking for him, that he was not angry with her. Surely, she thought now, if he was dead, she would know? Surely she would *feel* it?

Yes, Luc was alive. He had to be. In that moment, realising she could not live without him, Arianne made a decision. If she found Luc, if he was well enough to leave this evening to join the Maquis as he had planned, she would go with him. Her courage faltered as she remembered Father Julien's warning, but when she looked out of her bedroom window she saw only the village roofs and a tabby cat sunning himself on the garden wall. Samaroux looked as quiet as it ever had. She ran downstairs to pull her father's old rucksack from the wardrobe on the landing. Socks, underwear, a warm jersey. The family photograph from his desk, her toothbrush, the picture drawn for her in kindergarten by Paul – what else did one need for a life on the run? She threw in her candle, some matches and a pair of corduroy trousers.

The church bells began to ring for midday. Two storeys down, she heard the front door open. Paul, home for lunch! How was she going to explain this to him? *I'm sorry, I'll be back, one day you'll understand . . .* The bells stopped and she realised it was too early, Paul would only just be leaving school. The footsteps grew closer, too slow for her little brother. Who, then? Her bedroom door swung open.

☙

'So you're leaving,' said Elodie. She stood in the doorframe, her eyes on the rucksack Arianne clutched to her chest.

Arianne nodded.

'To look for the boy.'

'Yes.'

'They say it's him blew up that train.'

'That's not true.'

'I didn't say it was.'

Elodie sat, not without grace, on the edge of the bed. Arianne, after a moment's hesitation, sat beside her.

'I have to do this,' she said. 'I have to go.'

'France will stand or fall whether you stay home or not. But I suppose you are your father's daughter. Have you told your brother?'

'I haven't had the chance.'

'You thought you'd leave it to me to explain, you mean.'

The old lady's wrinkles broke into an unfamiliar smile. 'Sweet Lord, Arianne, I never dreamed when your father left you in my care just how difficult it would turn out to be.'

'We don't *mean* to be difficult.'

'You're wild, the pair of you.' Elodie reached out her hand. After a moment's incomprehension, Arianne took it in her own.

'I had a sweetheart myself, once.'

Arianne forced herself to be patient.

'What happened to him?' she asked.

'Oh, he married someone else. Mother wouldn't let me because he was going to Indochina.'

'Auntie I really have to . . .'

'I would have liked to go to Indochina. I heard he came home and retired near Angoulême. He's still there today, as far as I know, surrounded by his doting family. And here am I, with you two.'

'*We* love you . . .'

'Please. Love is complicated enough as it is without making a song and dance of things. So your brother's not home.'

'Not yet,' muttered Arianne.

'You know he skipped school again today.'

'What?'

'His teacher stopped by the presbytery during morning break. *I do hope Paul will be better soon*, she said. Pointedly.'

'But he promised!'

'Since when does he keep his promises? Arianne, you are fifteen years old and more of a child than you think, but I shan't try to stop you doing what you imagine is right. Just, before you go, think of your brother. I am old. I don't think I can manage him on my own.'

'You're blackmailing me!' cried Arianne.

'Yes,' said Elodie modestly. 'I believe I am.'

Arianne dropped her head to her knees and closed her eyes. 'It's not fair,' she said. 'Why do I always have to think of him?'

'Because you're all he has.'

The air in the bedroom where they sat was still, the light from the windows a pale grey which showed up the dullness of walls in need of painting. No sound here either, other than the occasional shout of a child making his way home for lunch, the sudden cackle of a magpie.

The clock struck the half hour. Arianne sat bent double over her knees. Paul then, not Luc. Not a new life of love on the run, but everything she had always known, domesticity and waiting. She hated for people to see her cry, but this time she could not stop herself.

'He might return,' said Elodie.

'And he might not.'

Into the silence of the stairwell came a new sound from outside, an unfamiliar sound they had somehow failed to notice while they were talking. Engines, not just one, but several. More than several – the wood of the stairs beneath Arianne's feet shook with the rumble of traffic.

'What *is* going on?' she thought she heard Elodie say, but she couldn't be sure because at the same moment they heard the back door flung open and the clatter of Solange running up the stairs shouting *Ari, Ari, it's too late, they're here!*

## II

Romy had ridden into Samaroux in the German convoy, two dozen *feldgrau* oblongs bristling with guns. It was lunchtime and the village was deserted. Behind the lace curtains and shutters half closed against the midday sun he imagined people rising from their kitchen tables to look at them, but nobody came out. Only Mayor Jarvis put down his soup spoon with a feeling of dread and reached for his jacket as the convoy ground to a halt across the market square from his home.

'I'm frightened,' he told his wife. She stood before him to straighten his tie, then helped him into his jacket.

'They won't stay long,' she said.

*They might!* he wanted to cry. *They might do anything.*

'I can always warm lunch for you when you come back.' She smiled and he saw that she too was afraid.

By the time Jarvis crossed the square the convoy had already split up. Two vehicles remained where they were, including the Captain's. Two returned to the entrance of the village. The rest were deployed around the village, to block the minor roads heading out towards the farms and hamlets.

'Routine inspection,' announced the Captain when Jarvis, having introduced himself, muttered offers of assistance. 'A few questions to ask. The boy here will show me around.'

Romy looked sick. Out of the corner of his eye Jarvis saw the curtain of the presbytery twitch and thought he caught a glimpse of the priest's bald pate. He felt a surge of anger towards his old friend.

'As mayor of this community,' he said with a firmness he did not feel, 'I insist upon accompanying you.'

'Ah well,' said the Captain, and Jarvis noted how Romy

shuddered at his voice. 'If you absolutely insist . . . You –' he pointed at Jo Dulac – 'get out. Give the man your place.'

Teresa Belleville knew they were coming. Ever since her son had told her last night that he was leaving, ever since she heard about the derailment this morning, she knew that they would come looking for him, with that conviction born of fear, the sort of fear only a parent can feel, which twists the guts and hollows the heart and makes them cry, when their worst nightmares are confirmed, I knew it! I knew no good would come of it! It was already the ghost of Teresa Belleville who opened her front door to the knock of the Captain's driver. The Captain asked his questions in German. Jonas Bucher acted as interpreter. Two more soldiers stood by the door.

'He has gone to visit my family in the south,' intoned Teresa.

'When did he get permission for this journey?'

'Yesterday.'

'Monsieur le maire, is this true?'

Jarvis, caught off guard, did not play his part well. He was not sure, he mumbled. There were so many applications to travel, so many permits required. He would have to check. Though yes, now he came to think of it, Luc had applied for permission to travel. It was all coming back to him, of course he had. He had a grandfather in Aix whom he loved very much.

The Captain slapped him. Jarvis's blue eyes filled with tears.

'You remember no such thing,' said the Captain, in French. The mayor did not contradict him.

The Captain nodded for his men to come forward.

'Where is your son?' he asked again.

Teresa started to cry with the second slap across her face, but did not budge from her story.

'He has gone to Aix.'

Slap.

'In the middle of term?'

'My father is ill.'

Slap.

'Why did you not go yourself?'

'I have not been well, I am not well enough to travel.'

She threw up when they punched her in the stomach, and soiled herself when they kicked her. When the Captain gave the order for the needles to come out, she admitted she was lying but refused to say where Luc had gone.

'I don't know.'

Bang went a needle under the nail of her left thumb.

'He wouldn't say.'

The index of her right hand.

'He was trying to protect me.'

The ring finger of her left hand, the one which still

bore her wedding band, and they could get no more out of her than screams.

It took less than fifteen minutes. By the time the Captain and his henchmen left, no wiser than when they arrived, Teresa Belleville was a rag upon the kitchen floor, blood seeping from her tortured hands and dry sobs shaking her body. Seated at her kitchen table, Jarvis wept. Jonas Bucher fumbled his way out of the house and threw up in the garden. Romy followed the Captain back to the jeep with the odd disjointed motions of a puppet.

This time when they passed through the village the windows of Samaroux were crowded with faces. Some people clenched their fists and made for their doors, but more people held them back, praying they would not be next. Father Julien slipped into his church and fell to his knees before the altar. Solange left her bedroom window, the one which looked straight into Teresa Belleville's home, slipped out of her parents' house and ran back to Arianne.

# Afternoon

## I

'Who are *they*?' demanded Elodie. 'What are you talking about?'

'Soldiers,' gasped Solange. 'Everywhere! They came to Luc's house, with the mayor and Romy.'

'*Romy?*'

'I saw them arrive from my bedroom window. You know I can see straight into their parlour. I was in my room, I was about to come back . . . They hit Monsieur Jarvis and then oh my God, oh my God, oh my God, Luc's mother! I knew I shouldn't have said anything!'

Solange burst into tears.

'Said what?' insisted Elodie. 'To whom?'

'Romy's father! He asked me where Luc was, I said I didn't know! But I didn't! I didn't know then!'

Arianne squared her shoulders.

'I'm going to see her.'

'You'll do no such thing,' snapped Elodie. 'You'll get out of this house this minute and hide. If they're after

Luc they'll come looking for you next. We'll get word to you somehow when it's safe.'

'But . . .'

'Hurry *up*, child, for heaven's sakes!'

Arianne reached for her rucksack. Elodie drew her into a brief and astonishing hug. 'God keep you,' she whispered.

'I'm sure you'll have words for Him if He doesn't.' Arianne tried to smile.

'Absolutely right. Now run before I . . .'

Two storeys down, someone hammered on the front door.

Elodie stifled Solange's scream with her hand. 'Roof,' she hissed at Arianne. She found time for another wry smile. 'Oh yes, I know about the roof. Solange, lock the window after her, then get back here and follow me downstairs. And let me do the talking. I won't have you spoiling everything with hysterics.'

Arianne shot out of the window. Solange twisted the handle shut after her and dashed for the stairs. She emerged into the kitchen with Elodie on her arm, every inch the concerned great-niece, just as the Captain's henchmen burst into the room.

Arianne crawled to the edge of the roof and stopped. An armed sentry stood beneath the holm oak on the street side. On the garden side the fields were crawling with soldiers. She crept back to the chimney stacks.

Curled into a ball, there was just room enough for her to hide.

## II

Paul stopped running as he came into Samaroux, slid out of the woods on to one of the minor roads, saw that it was blocked and slid right off it again. The long run had cleared his mind and he took his time thinking about what to do. If this road was blocked, it stood to reason that all the others would be too. So he would have to come in through the fields. He considered skirting around the village to come up through his own garden but it would take too long. The German convoy was well ahead of him but he didn't know yet if they had got to Arianne. In fact – he frowned – he knew nothing other than the few words the traitor Romy had told him. *The traitor Romy.* He rolled the words around his mind, his imagination feeding on what Elodie referred to with a sniff as *the wrong sort of comic*, picturing Romy's head on a spike, Romy hanging from a lamp post, Romy bound for the village stocks . . .

*Run and hide.* If he slithered down this bank, he would come out by the cemetery. The place gave him the creeps, but he'd scaled the wall often enough for a dare and at least it brought him out on the right side of the village. It meant going past school, but he'd cross that bridge when he came to it.

No time to stop at his mother's grave, but he crossed himself as he ran past the end of her row. He ran out through the little gate on the other side, smoothing down his hair to look halfway respectable, using the palm of his hand and a bit of spit to clean the fresh grazes on his knee. To his left, a German jeep barred the road out of town two hundred metres away. Further on, two more stood on either side of the market square. There was no one about save the soldiers in the vehicles, who clocked him, he was sure of that, but did not react. He made himself as small as possible as he walked past school but no irate teacher hauled him in. He began to breathe again when he reached the church, but froze when he turned the corner towards home.

Another jeep blocked the street, level with his house, and a guard stood posted beneath the old holm oak.

### III

Inside the house, Elodie was putting on a splendid show.

'Is this the girl?' The Captain nodded at Solange as the women entered the kitchen. Romy shook his head. Solange looked at him with open loathing. Elodie announced that she was rather busy and could anyone please tell her what was going on?

'*Where* is my niece? Where indeed?' she cried in response to Jonas Bucher's first question. 'I'd be grateful if anyone could tell me that!'

'She's bluffing,' said the Captain in German. 'Press her harder. And Bucher, for Christ's sake . . .'

'Sir?'

'Pull yourself together, man. You're shaking like a girl.'

Jonas cleared his throat, but Elodie ignored his attempts to tell her everything would go better if she just told the truth, and pressed on with her rant.

'Here am I, run off my feet, seventy-six years old and still struggling to support my nephew's children, and they cannot even bother to come back for lunch! And I issued clear enough instructions, believe me. Go to the butcher's, I said, then bake the sausage. But would madam listen? Oh no! It's all *I've got a day off school* and *I'm not your servant* and Miss Flibbertigibbet flutters off to goodness knows where, and here is her poor cousin come looking for her as well, hoping to spend the afternoon with her so they can catch up on their schoolwork . . .'

'If you could just tell us . . .'

'A nice *andouillette*, I told her, because I knew the butcher would have some today, but I come home and what do I find? A knuckle of ham, which I've yet to put on myself, and no hope of eating it until tonight and even then the peas won't have had long enough to soak!'

'It is imperative . . .'

'Christ!' said the Captain. 'What is it with these people and their food?' He pushed Jonas out of the way and came to stand before Elodie.

'Grandmother, we have to find your niece. She has been consorting with a known criminal. If you can't tell us where she is, we are going to have to search your house. If I find you have been lying to me, I will shoot you.'

'Shoot me anyway!' Elodie burst into tears, calculated that the Captain would not be receptive to physical contact and threw herself into Jonas's arms. 'Shoot me anyway, and spare me from these ungrateful children!'

'There, there.' Jonas patted her back. 'It's not so bad.'

'Known criminals!' sobbed Elodie. 'The *andouillette*! And her brother cutting school!'

She clutched at Solange, who led her away from Jonas Bucher to a seat at the kitchen table. Solange, feeling daring, allowed herself a reproachful look at the soldiers. The Captain grabbed her chin in his hand and forced her head back.

'Do you know where she is?' he demanded.

Solange's porcelain skin was flushed, her lower lip trembled with fear, but her wide blue eyes met his full on. He held them for a moment, and in the depths of his own eyes she read some unexpected light – not lust, not even contempt, something almost like regret. She shook her head. The light flickered and died.

'Search the house,' said the Captain.

They went up to her room, of course. Looked under her bed, ripped through her wardrobe, even emptied her chest of drawers. One of them rattled the window. Up above, Arianne stifled a moan.

'Low roof. She could have got out through there.'

'If she did, she's long gone. And anyway, it's locked.'

They tore through Paul's room and took his stash of cigarettes, through Elodie's wardrobe full of carefully mended dresses, through the untouched sanctum of her nephew's study.

'Nothing, sir.'

The Captain looked about him at the kitchen.

'My grandparents lived in the country,' he said. Again, the light in his eyes flickered and died.

'Ring the church bells,' he said. 'It's time to bring them in.'

IV

Alois led one of the parties to empty the neighbouring farms. He rode shotgun in an armoured jeep, rifle at the ready. His brow beneath the rim of his helmet was furrowed, his eyes half closed in apparent concentration, but his mind was somewhere else.

How different it was here from the east, he thought. These fields of green corn on which kernels of fruit were just beginning to ripen, these light woods of oak and elm and beech, these houses nestling in the landscape. Campion and buttercups blazed in the hedgerows. They passed an open meadow in which a herd of cows were grazing, and the smell of the farmyard hit him, the warmth of fresh milk, the tang of manure. He sucked it in and noticed that others in the jeep did the same. Nothing like the smell of cows, he smiled faintly, to stir memories of childhood. The beasts here had hides of caramel, soft hair which curled over their faces. They were different from the cows back home but their eyes were just as dumb. They turned their heads as the jeep bounced past. Some of the younger ones leaped away. One crapped. None of them stopped chewing. Such were the priorities of the animal kingdom, thought Alois. Perhaps this was why they made one think of childhood. They reminded one of a time when eating and crapping were all that mattered.

He could not remember when he last felt this peaceful. The villages in the eastern territories had been miserable affairs, their inhabitants even more so, the result of centuries of oppression, he supposed, the Communists taking over where the Tsars had left off. The weather couldn't have helped, either. Nor the sight of an invading army . . . The thought of the Russian winter made him shiver, and he tilted his head again to the rays of the French sun. One day, he told himself, he would come back here to visit with Clara and Wolf. She would lie on a rug in a meadow while he taught the boy to fish, they would sunbathe and picnic and everything would be all right again.

The jeep juddered to a halt and its occupants leapt to the ground. They had arrived at a farmhouse. Even now, with the adrenaline pumping through his veins and the rush of blood in his head, Alois noticed how moss and lichen clung to the tiles of the roof, enhancing the illusion that it seemed to be growing out of the ground. He bellowed an order for the occupants of the farm to come out. He shouted in German, and so loud it was barely comprehensible to his own men, but it didn't matter. His meaning was clear enough.

The farmers here were old and could not run. He shuffled out of his barn holding a spanner, she stepped out of the dairy with her head held high. A girl came out behind her, wiping her hands. Both wore scarves to tie back their hair and smelled of buttermilk and sweat.

'How many more?' demanded Alois in French.

The old farmer nodded towards a meadow adjoining the barn. An old farmhand walked towards them, leading a cow heavy with calf. He did not look at the soldiers.

'Any more?' asked Alois in French.

From inside the house, a baby began to wail. Alois tossed his head. The girl ran into the house and came back out with the child.

'Where's the father?'

'Gone to town,' spat the farmer. 'He'll not be back till evening.'

'Search the house.'

They made a thorough job of it. Ripped open cupboards, overturned beds, smashed through the pantry. Searched everywhere a man could have hidden, and many places where he couldn't. No sign of the son, of course. He'd probably made a run for it the minute he heard them coming. The soldiers spilled back out of the house. The farmer and his wife waited, resigned. The girl had turned away from them to nurse her baby, but she prised it off her breast when the men re-emerged, and buttoned up her dress. Bring them in, the Captain had said. Alois gritted his teeth and tried to ignore the child's whimpers.

'Village,' he said, with a toss of his head. 'Routine inspection.'

They stared back, as dumb as one of their cows. One of the men hit the farmhand with the flat of his gun, kneed him in the small of the back growling *allez*, go!

*Allez!* The word all French farmers use to get their cattle moving. They began to walk, the farmers very straight, the farmhand's head bowed in shame, the daughter-in-law with her fretting baby, walked away from their home along the unpaved track lined with wild flowers, looking for all the world as if they were going for a family walk, except for the jeep which followed. They crossed others on their way, farmhands working in the fields, children walking back to afternoon school. As the procession grew, the soldiers jumped down from the car to walk alongside them, guns cocked, missing nothing.

*Routine inspection*, said Alois whenever anybody asked.

He knew that he would never come here again.

## V

Picot had told Luc to keep a lookout while he rested in the armchair in the kitchen at Lascande, legs sprawled out before him, his rifle on his knees. Luc wasn't sure exactly *how* he was to keep watch, since Picot had forbidden him to go outside and also to open windows. Stripped to the waist, a blanket around his shoulders, he paced from room to room, peering out where he could through cracks in the shutters, before settling in the living room, from where he could just glimpse a corner of the drive.

'Who are you waiting for?' asked Baptiste.

The injured man lay behind Luc on the sofa, also

wrapped in a blanket, two of Madame Lascande's once pristine tea-towels pressed against his stomach wound.

'I bet it's a girl,' whispered Baptiste. 'No one ever looked so hopefully for the Milice.'

Luc moved away from the window.

'How are you feeling?' he asked.

'Great,' croaked Baptiste. 'For someone with a piece of train in his stomach.'

Luc scowled in the direction of the kitchen. 'He should have let me go for a doctor.'

'You know he couldn't do that, not in broad daylight. We got here too late. You were covered in blood. People would have noticed.'

'My shirt's almost dry now.'

'It's too late.' Baptiste tried to keep his eyes open but they fluttered shut. 'They'll be looking for you,' he whispered.

'I am going for a doctor,' said Luc through gritted teeth. 'And nobody is going to stop me.'

'Actually, you're coming with me.' Picot appeared in the doorway, rifle at the ready. 'Something's going on,' he said. 'We need to find out what.'

∞

Avoiding the main paths, Luc led Picot through the woods to the top of the hill above Lascande.

'What are we listening for?' he whispered.

'Engines.'

'I didn't hear anything.'

'Well I did.' Picot held up his hand. 'Shh!'

'Now what?'

'Bells. Can't you hear them? Listen!'

They broke out of the trees' cover and lay on the ground in the long grass.

'Church bells,' whispered Luc. 'Coming from Samaroux.'

Picot's eyes were glued to his field-glasses. 'Look down there.'

Luc looked, and saw a column of people walking before an army jeep, flanked by German soldiers. An old man stumbled. A young woman helped him up.

'Over there.'

Picot took the field-glasses back and trained them on to an armoured vehicle parked across the road which led from Lascande to the village. 'They've blocked it off. The whole countryside is crawling with them. Christ, that must have been close. We must be just outside their search radius.'

'What are they looking for?' asked Luc.

'Us,' said Picot.

In the silence which passed between the two men, everything was brought sharply into focus – the hum of insects, the sweet smell of the grass, the way it swayed in the wind high on the hill. The pealing bells calling the people of Samaroux home.

'I have to go,' said Luc.

'I can't let you do that.'

'I have to.'

Luc began to run, scrambling down the hill in a half-crouch, but Picot was fast on his feet and tackled him to the ground.

'If you go back there, they'll kill you.' Picot had one knee on Luc's chest, his hands around his throat. 'They'll kill you, but not before they've tortured you into telling them where we are. Don't think you'll be able to resist them, because you won't. And I am damned if I will let you and your misguided principles compromise the work that Baptiste and I are doing.'

'If you were a real hero,' gasped Luc, 'you would give yourself up as well.'

'Do you really think that would make a difference?'

Luc roared and elbowed Picot in the ribs. The older man grunted and twisted the boy round so that he lay on his front. He grabbed Luc by the hair and forced his head up until he gasped for breath.

'You're going nowhere,' he hissed.

&#8766;&#8766;

Back at Lascande, Picot kept his gun trained on Luc as he checked the living-room windows.

'All locked,' he said. 'I wouldn't try to break them. You'll only hurt yourself and you'd have to rip out the frames in order to open the shutters. I'm not tying you up because I want you to look after Baptiste.'

'You can't just leave us here! I'm supposed to show you the way!'

'I'm sure I'll manage without you.'

Picot backed out of the room, his gun still pointing at Luc, stepped outside and turned the key in the lock. Luc roared and threw himself at the door. When pounding on it proved futile, he took off his shoe and hurled it at a window-pane. The glass shattered. He began to hammer away at the frame.

'Luc?' Baptiste's voice was weak.

'What is it?'

'Please don't leave me.'

Luc sank to the floor and sobbed.

## VI

From where he was hiding behind a fire hydrant, Paul heard the Captain's jeep tear up the village street towards the market square. He looked back at home: Elodie and Solange appeared in the doorway, flanked by soldiers. His great-aunt made a big show of locking the front door. Solange was crying. Arianne was nowhere in sight.

There was no way he could get home, not with that sentry by the wall. Paul slipped after the others, moving in the shadows.

The loudspeakers started as he drew level with the church.

*All inhabitants of Samaroux to gather on the market square, I repeat, all inhabitants to gather on the market square.*

The voice grew louder. A tank – an actual tank! – was crawling up the road towards him, the soldier with the loudspeaker standing in the front. Behind it, Paul could see the street was full of people, soldiers banging on doors, villagers stumbling out of houses, some in slippers, one still wearing his napkin tucked into his collar. Four-year-old Felicia Brest marched out of her parents' house with her bowl and spoon and carried on eating as the swelling crowd shuffled towards the market square.

Sod this, thought Paul. A drainage ditch ran along the side of the church. He dropped into it. Nobody saw him.

There was a hollow here, just big enough for him. He knew it well, having discovered it a few years back hunting for a ball. At this time of year, the entrance was overgrown with nettles, and he was wearing short trousers. The tank was rumbling closer. He gave a yelp of pain as the nettles brushed his legs and rolled in. Clods of earth fell from the ceiling as the tank rolled overhead. He had grown in the months since he had been here last, and the walls of his shelter pressed against him.

The church bells started to ring.

❧

From her vantage point on the roof, Arianne saw what looked like all of Samaroux walking towards the market square. There were no gunshots, no beatings. She assumed they must be emptying the houses to look for Luc. They would move on when they realised he was not here, but she would get to Lascande before them. She tried not to think about his mother.

Her whole body ached from crouching. She shifted, dislodging a tile. It hung by one corner, wedged into place by a clump of moss. She nudged it back towards her with her foot and slipped it into her rucksack. Back against the chimney, she thought of what she would say to Luc. How would she tell him about Teresa? She saw herself arriving at Lascande, the relief on his face, felt his embrace, the stubble on his cheek, smelt his familiar smell. Where would she tell him? In the scullery with her back against the cool damp walls, or in the kitchen, on the old armchair without its springs? He would kiss her, would carry on kissing her as they made their way through the house, cupping her face in his hands, drinking her in, he would tell her he always knew that she would come, he would lead her upstairs to the four-poster bed with its velvet curtains – she would *have* to tell him by then. She felt ashamed of her next thought, that perhaps after all this he would not leave. Perhaps he would just lie low for a while and return when the fuss had died down, to look after his mother. The price to pay for keeping him.

The loudspeakers were starting again. Arianne strained forwards as far as she dared to listen.

## VII

The Captain thrust a loudspeaker at Jonas Bucher.

'Loud and clear, soldier. If I hear your voice shake, I'll have you court-martialled. Ready?'

'Sir?'

'I'm promoting you to official interpreter. What's the name of this lad we've been looking for?'

'Luc Belleville, sir, I think.'

'Here goes then. People of Samaroux! Last night a terrible crime was committed against the Army of the Third Reich by a member of this community. His name was Luc Belleville.' The Captain stared at Bucher. 'Well? What are you waiting for?'

'Gens de Samaroux,' stammered Jonas. 'La nuit dernière un crime terrible a été commis...'

'Not to me, soldier,' snarled the Captain.

'Un crime atroce a été commis la nuit dernière contre l'armée du troisième reich!' bellowed Jonas, turning to the crowd. 'Par – euh – Luc Belleville.'

'I want you to tell me where he is.'

'Je veux que vous me disiez où il est.'

'This boy . . .' the Captain nodded towards Romy, and a soldier pushed him forward, 'has helped me. Now it is your turn. I'm sure you know the rules. If I cannot find the culprit, somebody must pay.'

Romy stood before the crowd with his face drained of colour and a cold sweat bathing his palms. The crowd stared back, hostile, but Gaspard Félix, the butcher, stepped forward.

'Sometimes,' he mumbled, 'I mean often, he likes to roam the woods.'

'We've searched the woods, fool.' The Captain answered Félix directly, and the crowd stirred at the revelation that he spoke French. '*Where* does he go?'

The butcher gulped and wiped his hands on his apron.

'I've got men beating the woods in a three-kilometre radius. How much further do you propose I go?'

Gaspard Félix trembled.

'How much *time* do you propose I devote to the hunting of this wretch? Answer me!'

'I don't know, sir.'

'You don't know.'

The Captain seized the butcher by the collar and dragged him to the top of the church steps. He gestured for Jonas Bucher to follow him.

'It is obvious to me that Luc Belleville did not act alone.'

'Il m'est évident que Luc Belleville n'a pas agi seul,' yelled Jonas.

'I am giving the accomplices of Luc Belleville the chance to step forward now. I will count to twenty. If nobody comes forward, this man will be shot.'

'Je vais compter jusqu'à vingt. Si personne ne se manifeste, cet homme sera exécuté.'

Monsieur Félix began to cry.

'So count, soldier,' sighed the Captain.

'Me?' said Jonas.

'No, you incompetent fool, Father Christmas. He's standing right behind you.'

*One, two, three, four . . .*

The soldiers on the edge of the square kept their guns trained on the crowd. The people of Samaroux shifted. From where he stood, Alois saw how some of the younger men eyed the soldiers from beneath lowered lids, assessing their chances. *Do not run,* he muttered under his breath. *You fools, whatever you do, do not run.*

*. . . nine, ten, eleven, twelve . . .*

Father Julien finished saying his prayers and stepped forward on the count of fifteen.

*. . . sixteen, seventeen, eighteen, nineteen . . .*

On the count of twenty, Romy joined him.

## VIII

The loudspeaker on the market square had stopped. The clock struck the hour. Three o'clock, and the air was still. Arianne strained forward to listen. A lark rose from the fields behind her, and she was struck by the fancy that if she reached out far enough, if she could just stand on tiptoe on the ridge pole, she might be able to touch it.

The lark's song faded, carried on the breeze.

## IX

We are no longer ourselves, the Captain once told Alois in a Belorussian stable. This was how he justified his actions. It was not he who ordered his men to fire the machine guns which sent the first five hundred into the gravel pit. Not he who walked among the dying and the dead, shooting any body that moved, or who gave the act of ethnic cleansing the rules and structure of a blood sport. Not he, not really he, who stood before the massed villagers of Samaroux on the market square on this quiet day in early summer, staring at a village priest and a boy.

'How very . . . unimaginative,' he said. 'The priest with a taste for self-sacrifice and the traitor with a conscience.'

A look passed between the two before him. The priest nodded a fraction before turning to the Captain.

'We two are responsible.'

'The boy who stands beside you now betrayed you earlier.'

'And now he is paying the price.'

'I know what you people do to those who betray you, you so-called Résistants. You're as merciless as the rest of us. Don't pretend you don't want to tear him to pieces.'

'God tells us to forgive.'

'God also tells you not to kill, but that didn't stop your lot last night.'

'We are angry.'

'So am I,' growled the Captain. 'But at least I'm not a hypocrite.'

'Not a hypocrite, no.' Father Julien smiled. 'Though I think, perhaps, you are the devil.'

'I don't believe you,' hissed the Captain. 'I don't believe this child was responsible for what happened to my men, I don't even know what this lad we've been chasing has to do with it. But someone has to pay. I'll show you what the devil can do.'

As two privates hustled Father Julien into the church, Alois had a fleeting vision of a different scenario – anarchy, the Captain annihilated, the morning's explosion forgotten as the army of the Third Reich roared northwards towards home. They would cross the border in secret, mend roofs, tend livestock, hide until the end of the war. They would become human again.

The vision did not last long.

'Time for plan B,' murmured the Captain, and as Alois's vision faded he saw that the boy Romy was back in the crowd and that his father was holding him by the hand. He could not avoid this, then. There had never been any other plan, only this one, the one they had rehearsed so many times before in the villages of Eastern Europe.

'Time for plan B,' repeated the Captain, and fired his gun to give the signal.

X

They were coming back! If she craned her neck enough, Arianne could just make out the edge of the market square where a column of children stood in a crocodile along the wall of the church. No sign of Paul but that didn't mean anything from this distance. She shuffled to her right. The ranks of women came into view and she saw – she was almost sure – Elodie's crown of grey curls, the bright pattern of Solange's dress.

They were coming down the street. Thierry, Marc, Jérôme and a dozen other men she knew, but why were there soldiers with them? A dozen of them, carrying rifles, with more following with heavier equipment.

'Halt!' They stopped in front of her house and she drew back. She heard another order, but did not understand it. Her first thought was to run. What with the cries of protest from the village men, the shouted orders, the repeated slamming into the garden door, it was possible they would not hear her . . . She had stuffed her shoes in her rucksack before climbing out of the window. The thing was to do it *now*, while they could not see her.

They were kicking in the broken door in the wall, the door beside the holm oak which led into the old dog run beneath her. She heard the sound of breaking glass, and the group of men she had seen walking down the street were herded in – she recognised Thierry's voice as he intoned the Marseillaise.

'Silence!' shouted a German voice.

'Oh go to hell,' said Thierry, but the singing stopped.

Arianne risked a look behind her. Other men were being marched down the street. She recognised Sol's father, Gaspard Félix and farmer Legros. She thought she heard a cry to halt as they drew level with the Renault garage, and watched with mounting dread as they were pushed inside.

Something terrible is going to happen, she thought. Soldiers were pouring in from everywhere. They were wheeling heavy machines down the street, machines which looked like . . .

*I can stop this. They are looking for Luc. I can help them find him.*

The moment she thought it she knew it was the right thing to do. *Quick, now, before you change your mind* . . . she remembered Solange's words from earlier as she scrambled to her feet. Quick, now! Turn him in, turn yourself in! Tell them what you know!

A volley of shots rang out and the world exploded.

She felt the house shake beneath her under the impact of the machine guns. She covered her ears to block out the screaming, closed her eyes and clamped her mouth on to the fabric of her dress. The screaming gave way to moans. Arianne pressed her fingers harder into her ears and tried to pray.

No words came, only images. Her father nursing his pipe, her mother's hair against the white of her pillow, Luc on the terrace at Lascande with a tray of tea and biscuits . . . There were new sounds now, grunting and shuffling as bodies were dragged across the dog run into the house. Arianne stuffed her fists into her mouth.

Luc's eyes, Luc's mouth, Luc's smile . . . the images no longer came.

The moaning had finished and now she could hear whooping and the sound of engines. A jeep screeched to a stop by the house. Down below, she caught a glimpse of a soldier spreading straw around the dog pen. Somebody laughed.

They were burning everything. Smoke was rising, around the village, around her. It carried the smell of kerosene and something else, acrid and sweet and nauseating at once. Soldiers were still gathered in the road below her, shouting words she did not understand. Sparks flew up around her and the smoke grew thicker. She could no longer see the street but the soldiers' voices were growing more distant as they made their way back to the market square.

They had gone. No one saw Arianne as she crept off her perch and half crawled over the roof, or heard her cry as she threw herself off. She landed badly but ran barefoot over grass and gravel until she reached the edge of the orchard. There was a gap in the old stone wall where the foundations had collapsed. Elodie was always complaining about it, ever since the deer had broken in. Arianne threw herself through it. Brambles tore at her arms and caught at her rucksack. She shrugged it off her shoulders and glanced back.

No one had come after her. She yanked herself out of

the brambles and fell on to the grass, nursing her swelling ankle.

## XI

Paul considered every part of his body, focusing on a few square inches at a time, and concluded that everything hurt. His neck and shoulders ached from not being able to sit straight, his legs had gone dead, his back was stiff and his arms were covered in nettle rash. Worst of all – and this had almost driven everything else from his mind – his bladder was stretched to bursting point. He had passed the point of nearly wetting himself, and moved on to a throbbing cramp which made him worry that he was doing some serious damage to his tackle. Sounds were muffled in his underground bunker. He had been aware of somebody shouting through a loudspeaker, then of somebody counting. A gunshot right above him made him leak a little. He tried to listen more carefully then, but it was very quiet. He manoeuvred himself round so that he could lie on his side with his shorts undone, pointing into the grass outside his lair. The Captain's second gunshot sped things up and everything felt better. He rolled his shoulders just a little, and wriggled his toes to get some feeling back into his legs.

His sense of relief did not last long. As he became aware of the dampness of the ground beneath him – he had not succeeded, then, in peeing outside his den – he heard the sound of wailing. Now that the blood was not pounding in his ears he could hear muffled gunshots – not directly above him, like last time, but further away towards the village, though hard to make out where with all the screaming. His stomach cramped and he worried that now he might soil his pants. It was cold beneath the ground. He pulled his knees up towards his chest and wrapped his arms around them. He tried to blink back his tears. Then, realising there was no one to see him, he let them fall.

## XII

Some of the women tried to break away. One, with a baby on her hip and a toddler clinging to her hand, had to be struck several times before she understood she could not go home. Her little girl began to scream. The woman hoisted her on to her free hip and joined the throng being herded into the church.

'What are they doing?' stammered Jonas. 'Why are they going into the church?'

'Well it's not to pray, is it?' said Alois through gritted teeth. The young soldier's panic was getting to him. He wanted to tell him to find someone else to stick to, except that none of the other men could be trusted not to shoot him. With the exception of the new recruit, they all wore the same expression, one he knew only too well. Eyes glazed, faces shining, they were wound so high one wrong word from Bucher could be the end of him.

'Just do as you're told,' muttered Alois. 'And for Christ's sake stop asking questions.'

A wooden rattle rolled out from the sea of feet. A child ran after it, a girl with round limbs and pudgy knees and tangled hair falling into her eyes. Jonas leaned down to pick up the toy. Alois willed him not to look at her but it was too late. Jonas and the girl were smiling at each other.

'I've got a sister,' said Jonas.

'Stop!'

A figure was fighting its way out of the church, pressing against the crowd. The priest, his black robes covered in dust, struggling to walk with his hands tied behind his back. *Damn*, thought Alois. *What the hell were we supposed to do with him?*

'I will not allow this!' The old man spoke passable German, for a Frenchman.

'I'm not in charge,' said Alois.

'Find me the one who is!'

The Captain came. The priest stumbled free of the crowd and emerged on the front steps. His cassock was torn, his cheek badly grazed. He had lost his glasses. He blinked, looking lost.

'You,' said the Captain. 'I'd forgotten about you.'

'What are you doing with these women and children?'

'They're going to church, father. Perhaps you could read them a lesson.'

'Why?'

The Captain shrugged and waved his arm towards the burning village. 'Where else can they go? What was it our Lord said before he died? *I will prepare my father's house for you.*'

'Don't you dare quote scripture at me!' spat the priest.

'I don't have time for this,' sighed the Captain.

'I will not let you deface the house of God.'

'Fine.' The Captain turned to Jonas and Alois. 'Private Bucher, shoot the priest.'

'I . . .'

'Do it!'

The priest fell to his knees. Alois turned away but out of the corner of his eye he saw the old man murmur as he crossed himself, and felt a grudging respect.

'These are innocent people,' said the priest. 'God will have retribution.'

'There are no innocents in war,' said the Captain. 'Only winners and losers. Now, please, Private Bucher.'

Jonas screamed and fired. Father Julien fell to the ground, his body bouncing under the impact of a second bullet.

⁊

Fifty soldiers stood around the church, their rifles trained on every exit. A dozen more pushed the last women and children into the building while two soldiers placed a large box in the middle of the central aisle and lit the strings which trailed from it. The box exploded, belching gas. The last of the fleeing soldiers slammed the doors shut.

The walls of the church were a metre thick in places. From where Alois stood the sound of the screaming inside was muted. He saw a figure appear at a window and watched it topple back into the building under a volley of bullets.

'Too slow,' said the Captain.

His men smashed more windows and hurled in incendiary grenades, threw open the doors to machine gun the crowd. When they were sure there were no survivors, they piled straw and poured paraffin over the bodies and set them alight.

As he watched black smoke billow up into the sky, Alois knew that it was carrying what was left of his soul to hell.

## XIII

Paul heard somebody whimper, closer than the screaming from the church, and realised that the noise was coming from him. He cried properly then, real sobs, not caring if anyone heard him. A timber from the roof crashed into his ditch and he howled. Smoke began to fill his den.

Every spring, Elodie smoked out the moles which wreaked havoc in her garden.

'They have to come out,' she explained. 'Or they will suffocate.'

'But when they come out, you will kill them.'

'They don't know that. They care only about the most immediate danger.'

Anger swelled from deep within him, breathing life back to his cramped limbs. That it should come to this! Cowering below ground like a helpless blind creature, smoked out by the Nazi equivalent of his great-aunt! There was no room in the den for Paul and his fury. To hell with the soldiers, their tanks and their guns. To hell with the burning church and whatever else was going on out there! Paul erupted on to the market square with a bellow of rage, ready for anything. Through the smoke, he made out the shapes of soldiers with guns. Guns which had been trained on the church but which now were all on him. He turned and saw more men behind him. He froze. So did they. There was no way out.

Footsteps, and the smoke appeared to dissipate around the figure of a single man who strode towards him out of the grey, flanked by another soldier and the giant he remembered from the lake.

The leader stopped a few feet from Paul and examined him gravely. The big man did not look at him. The boy – Paul saw now that he was just a boy, only a little older than Luc – appeared to have been crying. He registered the fact without emotion, then dragged his eyes back to the leader.

'Well,' said the Captain. 'What the hell do we have here?'

≈≈

The Captain, Alois knew, was close to breaking point. He knew it from the feverish glint in his eyes, and the tone of his voice, which for all its calm bordered on the hysterical. The slight frown, the pursed lips testified to his anger towards the people and circumstances which had allowed this to happen. The kid would have to be dealt with. Someone would have to kill him, but the solitary killings were always the hardest. Especially when the target was a child. Orders were orders, but everyone had a limit.

The Captain cleared his throat. 'Private Bucher.'

'Sir?' Jonas sounded as if he were dying.

'Nothing.' It seemed even the Captain had a conscience. 'Alois, I don't suppose you ...'

'No, sir.'

'Even if I order you ...'

'I'm sorry, sir.'

'What difference,' murmured the Captain, 'can one more make?'

'I won't shoot a child in cold blood, sir.'

Together they stared at the boy. He was filthy, his face streaked with dirt, his limbs covered in scratches, his clothes torn, his extraordinary red hair matted with grime. He half crouched before them like a cornered animal.

'I suppose it *is* a child,' mused the Captain. 'Though it hardly looks like one. Where did it come from? Underground?'

'I believe so, sir.'

'But *people* don't live underground, Alois. *People* live in houses. *Animals* live underground. That's completely different.'

'With respect, sir, this child is not an animal.'

'When did you last talk to a child, Alois?'

'A long time ago, sir.'

'Hardly an expert then, are you? Private Bucher!'

'Sir!'

'Explain the rules of play to the prisoner.'

'He doesn't know the rules, sir.'

'Well, then you tell Private Bucher, Alois, and he can translate. Is he or is he not my official interpreter?'

Alois took Jonas to one side to explain. 'I won't do it,' said Bucher. He began to cry again. 'You can't make me.'

'I'll deal with *him* later,' said the Captain when Alois reported back.

He led the boy to the centre of the square himself. From a distance, there was something almost intimate about the sight. The way they walked, with the Captain leaning forward, his hand on the boy's shoulder, the boy's face raised towards him – they could have been father and son out for a Sunday morning stroll.

'All done.' The Captain walked back to Alois's side. 'I told him to make for the far wall. I think it's best if we focus on that one. If he gets past it, we let him go. I said he shouldn't go back towards the village, there are too many houses burning, it would be dangerous.'

'*Dangerous?*'

'And I also told him it's only me who'll be shooting. That's fair, isn't it? To be honest, I don't think the men would be too happy if I asked them. I mean, *you* don't want to do it, and you're completely used to this sort of thing.'

'Used to it . . .'

'Alois, I do believe you're going senile in your old age.' The Captain drew his pistol from his belt. 'On my count, give the signal. And for God's sake stop repeating everything I say.'

Before the Occupation there was probably an animal fair on the village square on the first Saturday of every month, just like there was at home. Children would have petted horses and wet-nosed calves just separated from their mothers, chickens would have squawked in cages. There would have been bartering and negotiation, the smell of dung and fried food, the cries of cowmen and horse traders. But now there were several dozen soldiers on the edge of the square, indistinguishable from each other through the smoke. Burning buildings on three sides. A boy standing straight as an arrow in the centre, his eyes trained on the wall of the only house not burning. Three men standing together. One with a pistol, another with a rifle, the third with his face in his hands. No sound but the crackling of fire.

'One,' said the Captain, and Alois raised his pistol.

*The boy had been the same age as Wolf, and when they found him he was frozen solid . . .*

'Two.'

The wind picked up, blowing fat clouds across the summer sky. A shaft of sunshine pierced the pall of smoke which hung over the square. Sun danced on ash, a pillar of light.

'Three.'

*Clara. Her name meant light.*

The Captain could hit a running rabbit from the back of a galloping horse. He could hit a single starling mid-flight. Once, after a vodka-induced argument in Belorussia, he had shot a button off another officer's tunic from forty paces, before passing out cold for fourteen hours. The square was wide open. The kid didn't stand a chance.

A cloud scudded over the sun. The pillar of light vanished only to reappear stronger than before when the cloud moved on. The Captain stood a few feet before him, but his eyes were trained on the boy. The pistol felt heavy in Alois's hand. He raised it slowly. It would be so easy . . . so easy . . .

'For Christ's sake, Alois, what are you waiting for?'

'I . . .'

'You!' The Captain barked at one of the privates on the edge of the square. 'Give the signal.'

'Sir!'

And the private's pistol cracked, and the boy was running, and the Captain had taken his first shot. He missed by inches. On purpose, of course. He reloaded. His face was flushed. He was laughing. He was not here any more, but on the heathlands of home, shooting hare, pheasant, deer. There was no sign now of the man close to breaking point.

The Captain was enjoying himself.

His rifle was pressed against his cheek. The boy was fast. Two chances left, if he was quick about it. His finger was on the trigger, squeezing.

The sun grew brighter. A sob broke through Alois Grand's lips. He dropped his gun. The boy, with an uncanny sixth sense, swerved to the right as the bullet whistled past him. The Captain swore.

The pillar of light was burning now, but nobody else appeared to see it. It swayed gently as the breeze blew through the swirling ash giving it, for a fleeting moment, the shape of a woman.

*A woman dancing. A woman beckoning. A woman smiling upon him with forgiveness in her eyes, telling him what to do.*

The line of the Captain's cheek, smooth against the wooden rifle butt. Two bales of hay in a stable, a half-drunk bottle of vodka. A forest clearing, a bonfire for the dead. A gramophone record playing Puccini.

The index finger of a manicured hand, pulling back a trigger. The long pale fingers of Clara as she worked. A single rose on his son's bedside table.

Alois howled and threw himself against the Captain.

# Evening

Baptiste had died hours ago.

Luc sat on the floor with his back against the wall, watching him. There was no light coming through the chink in the shutters anymore.

*Soon,* he thought. *Soon, I will break out and go.*

He tried to move but his limbs would not obey him.

Footsteps. His body came to life and he was on his feet, bolting to hide behind the door, straining to listen. Whoever was there had a key. There was no sound of a door being forced, but someone was walking down the passage towards the kitchen, was in the kitchen now. Someone walking slowly with dragging steps, someone crying, someone calling out in a very small voice.

'Luc?'

'Ari!' he bellowed. 'Oh my Christ! Ari! I'm in here!'

༄

In the big bedroom at Lascande, Arianne sat curled in Luc's lap in one of the gilt-edged armchairs. Their eyes were red from crying, their arms locked around each other. She tried to move but he would not let her go. She pulled his head to her shoulder and pressed her cheek to his hair.

'It was my fault,' he whispered.

'No,' she murmured. 'No, no, no.'

He got up and walked over to the window.

'Don't open it,' she begged.

'No one's going to come now.'

He leaned his hands on the sill.

'What should we do?' he asked.

'I don't know. You're shivering. Come away from the window.'

She coaxed him towards the bed then limped to the bathroom, where she washed in freezing water. He was asleep when she returned. She lit a candle and placed it in a lamp, then pulled the covers up around him and dropped kisses on his closed eyelids, just as she remembered her mother doing to her. He stirred and she tiptoed away carrying her lamp, back to the gilt-edged armchair where she sat and stared into the night.

Out in the woods, Paul stumbled, moonlight on his flaming hair. Every inch of him was filthy and his face was streaked with tears. He did not think of where he was going, but he knew that there was only one place. A bend appeared in the road and he saw the iron gates, standing ajar. He slipped through them, still keeping to the shadows. In the window at the end of the house he saw his sister's lantern.

The forest was dark and still. Paul stopped for a moment and breathed it in. Then he squared his shoulders and walked the small remaining distance towards the light.

*Who knew that once you died you could see so clearly?*

*Samaroux burned on long after the soldiers left. Hours dead, and I saw everything. I saw the rats and crows nosing around the few corpses which had not been set alight, the dogs hungry for their evening meal. I saw the body of Alois Grand, killed by the bullet meant for Paul, and I saw Jonas Bucher and the pistol with which he took his own life. I saw a man crawl out of the cornfield where he hid when they took his family, and I saw villagers returned from town, bawling like babies. I saw my parents, my school-friends, my neighbours. All dead. I saw Arianne and Paul and Luc, crying in the big house at Lascande.*

*I could have loved him too. Oh, not like she does! She'll love him till the day she dies. Me, I just fancied him. I saw him from my bedroom window and I thought, I'd like some of that. Those cheekbones, those lips! That breath of fresh air, straight up from the south! We could have had fun. I wish we had. I wish . . .*

*Mainly I wish that I were still alive.*

*We might have stopped it too, Romy and Father Julien and I. We all knew where Luc was hiding, or at least where he was heading to. We could have led them straight there, but we didn't. I wonder if it would have made a difference?*

*I think about a lot of things, now that I am alone. Our lies and betrayals, our quarrels and silences, our messy sacrifices. I think of all the things we do for love.*

*I think about Luc and Arianne together at Lascande, and about what it means to be a hero.*

*I think that I loved her and I'm glad she's still alive.*

*I think, I did not want to die.*

☙

*I should leave now.*

*I should follow the others. Mother and Father and Elodie, Thierry and Marc and Jérôme, Father Julien and Mayor Jarvis and Monsieur Félix. Romy and Alois and Jonas. They've all gone. There's only me left now.*

*The liberating armies never did come to Samaroux when the war ended. What would have been the point? They marched down other village streets, down boulevards strewn with flowers, cheered by girls who fell in love and children hopeful for sweets, while the pavement here vanished under grass and dirt. Those who do come walk our streets in silence, and the flowers they bring are for our common grave. Alois's wife came, with her little boy. Monsieur Félix's son, returned from fighting with the Allies. Joseph Dupont's brother, whose name is really Golstein and who escaped to England at the beginning of the war. And Arianne.*

*She came with her father and Paul and Luc. Her father drove them in a second-hand Citroën with a Bordeaux number plate. Bordeaux, where her mother studied! Close enough to remember, far enough to forget. She wore a new dress and she looked so pretty.*

*They all cried except her. My uncle fell to his knees in the dirt and howled, and Luc cried quietly in front of the church. Paul made straight for his old house, climbed into the ruins of it and refused to come out, but Arianne came to the graveyard. She laid wild carnations on her mother's grave and then she came to us and sat on the grass right where we are all buried together.*

*'Hello, Sol,' she said.*

*That was all, but it was enough. She sat for a long time, and through her silence I felt everything. Her grief, her confusion. Her hopes, too, for the future. I like to think it helped her, coming back. I like to think she felt me too.*

*And then she also left.*

*I should stay. Who would speak for us, if I went too? Years from now when people stray here, I could tell this place's secrets. Stop a while, I could whisper to them. See how the shadows sway in the breeze? Children were born here, fought and made up. People loved and laughed and died. It wasn't always like this. Stop a while, and I will tell this place's story.*

*But then again . . . the sky is bright and beckoning and I am quite alone. Where once I had a body I now see earth and trees and stone. I have become insubstantial as the air and I find I do not mind.*

*It is time for me to leave this place.*

*It is time for me to go.*

# Afterword

My book is a story, my characters fiction. But on 10 June 1944, at around 2 o'clock in the afternoon, the 2nd SS Panzer Division Das Reich really did enter the French village of Oradour-sur-Glane and ordered all the inhabitants to assemble on the market square, under the pretext of checking their papers. What happened next was much as I described it. The men were separated from the women and children, taken to selected locations and shot. The women and children were herded into the church. When attempts to asphyxiate them failed, the church was set on fire.

Nobody during the eventual trials or in the years of study and examination which followed has ever understood why this happened. There was no train crash in real life, no Resistance activity. Only a quiet village, minding its own business, hopeful that soon the war would end. Theories abound. One of the more popular is that Oradour-sur-Glane was confused with another village some distance away, Oradour-sur-Vayres, where the Resistance were more active. Another is that the Allied landings in the North panicked the occupying forces, and that this massacre was no more than a flexing of muscles, a reprisal for the kidnapping of a German officer somewhere nearby the previous day. Oradour was small and contained enough to destroy with just a handful of men – 150 soldiers to 642 villagers.

The handful of villagers who did survive speak of unbelievable cruelty: of villagers being shot in the legs and then burned alive. Of the wounded being stuffed down wells. They say the flames in the church were so hot they melted the great bronze bell. But two details in the accounts I have read stood out for me amongst the orgy of killing. A small boy, emerging from hiding, shooed away by a young German soldier into the woods and safety. And the description of another young soldier sobbing by the side of the road that evening, when the first witnesses arrived at Oradour to find out what was going on. I'm not sure if it makes it better or worse to be reminded of the human side of the men who committed such barbaric murder, but that is the side I chose to focus on in my novel. Alois's sacrifice for Paul is a small act of atonement in the face of such unimaginable horror, but it offers him, and us, a much-needed glimmer of redemption

Today, the village has been turned into a museum. The visit begins in a purpose built Centre of Remembrance, which explains the events which led up to that fateful day. From there, you proceed to the village, which has been left exactly as it was. Nothing has been rebuilt. Cars sit rusting in fields overgrown with flowers, buildings slowly crumble. There is the twisted frame of a pram in the church. At various points in the village – in barns and garages and, most horribly, by a well – signs urge you to be mindful of the men who died here. All around, people talk in whispers. Many are moved to tears. It may be a cliché, but Oradour is one of those places where everywhere you turn there are ghosts. Step away from the crowd for a moment, slip into a house or the graveyard, touch one of those rusting cars, and if you have a speck of imagination you can see it as it used to be.

If you want to know more about the events of 10 June 1944, there is plenty of information available in English on the Internet – just search for 'Oradour sur Glane'. Or, of course, you can visit the Centre de la Mémoire (Centre of Remembrance), which is located 20 kilometres west of Limoges (www.oradour.org). I promise you'll never forget it.

NF
London, 8 September 2011